CALL TO ARMS

A DETECTIVE KAY HUNTER CRIME THRILLER

RACHEL AMPHLETT

SAXON
PUBLISHING

ONE

Ten years ago

East of Maidstone, Kent

Jamie Ingram stalked across the darkened farmyard, shoved the crash helmet onto his head, and swung his leg over the motorbike.

He sat for a moment, his heart racing, anger coursing through his veins.

He realised he was grinding his teeth, and he forced his jaw to relax. He leaned forward, flexed his fingers over the handlebars, then started the engine and kicked the bike into gear.

It had been raining since four o'clock that afternoon, a steady downpour that soaked the landscape and had continued into the night. A weak full moon attempted to break through the clouds that tumbled overhead, then submitted to the next deluge.

The Kentish countryside held a starkness to it, tree branches reaching up to the pitch black sky while the promise of an early morning frost clung to the air around him.

A chink of light appeared at one of the upper windows to the farmhouse, before the silhouette of a man emerged.

Jamie remained still, glaring through the visor, his breathing ragged.

As a boy, he had loved waking up to the sound of rain as it beat upon the roof of the house. The crops were dependent on the ebb and flow of the seasons, and despite the risk of flooding, he found the noise soothing.

Tonight though, it seemed to heighten his frayed nerves instead.

Eventually, the figure retreated and the curtain at the window dropped back into place.

Jamie blinked to regain his night vision.

He turned the bike's wheels in the mud that now

coated his boots and pointed it towards the cattle grid separating the property from the lane.

The farm hadn't been home to animals for nearly two decades, but the cattle grid served as a makeshift security measure – the rumble of tyres across its steel bars could be heard from within the farmhouse, giving its occupants ample time to see who was arriving.

He checked for oncoming traffic before accelerating into the road from habit rather than necessity. He didn't expect to see anyone – it was the dead of night, after all, and the only people who used the road were the residents of the farmhouse and tenants from a couple of cottages further along.

The high banks and hedgerows either side of the lane sheltered him from the worst of the wind that tried to batter the motorcycle, but did little to protect him from the fresh onslaught of rain that now streaked across the fields.

On any other night, he'd have resisted the urge to be out riding.

The phone call had put paid to that.

He growled under his breath, and leaned the bike into the first bend.

A cold chill crawled over his shoulders as fear began to overcome his anger.

It wasn't meant to be like this.

Everything was out of control.

The phone conversation had begun with accusations, and deteriorated from there.

He had paced while he spoke, gesticulating with one hand as he tried to placate the person on the other end of the call.

It was too dangerous. They had to stop.

It couldn't continue – not anymore.

The caller was insistent; there was too much at stake, too many promises made.

He slowed the motorbike as he approached a T-junction, checked his mirrors, and took a moment to roll his shoulders and crick his neck.

Tension clutched at his limbs, and he briefly closed his eyes. A wave of nausea seized him, cramping his stomach.

He reached up and flipped the visor open, gulping in the fresh air, fighting the dizziness that clawed at the periphery of his vision.

Rain pecked at his face, and he savoured the cold water that helped to soothe his burning cheeks.

He had berated the caller for making the promises in the first place. That hadn't been the arrangement.

They had always known they were on borrowed time, and he wasn't prepared to take the risk.

Not now. He'd already lost so much.

He took a deep breath, and tried to refocus, clenching his gloved hands to try and wring the tension from them. He reached up and replaced the visor, the Perspex muting the soft undertones of damp earth and ozone, cocooning him from reality.

There was only one person he could speak to who would know what to do.

He wrapped his fingers around the handlebars once more.

He swivelled his head to check for oncoming traffic, and wasn't surprised when the lane stayed deserted.

Only a fool would be out on a night like this.

Surface water glistened in the light from the headlamp, and he took advantage of the fact that he was the only one on the road and swerved between the deep puddles, using the width of the lane to manoeuvre.

His heart raced as if he'd been running, and he wondered if he had made the right choice. There was no turning back now – when he had made the decision, it had been an automatic knee-jerk reaction. He had been pushed too far, too fast.

What he had first viewed as a bit of a laugh and then a challenge had instead turned into something he had no control over. There were too many others involved now.

The road dipped and curved as the terrain levelled out. A familiar sign glowed in the headlight beam to his left, and he began to slow the machine using the gears rather than risk applying the brakes too hard.

The main road was deserted, and as he approached the junction a flash of movement between the trees beyond his position caught his eye. A moment later, a Eurostar train flashed by, its pantograph sending bright bolts of electricity through the air as it powered its way towards the coast and onwards to Paris.

A dull sensation clawed at Jamie's chest.

He would give anything to be out of the country again right now.

Resigned, he turned onto the A20 and steered the bike in the direction of Maidstone.

As the gradient began to rise, he lined up to take the corner; it was easy – he'd been riding the route since he had left school and got his licence. His body and the machine moved as one, leaning into the curve as he accelerated to control the turn.

His brain registered the dark shape that loomed in front of him a fraction too late.

Desperate, he pushed the left-hand handlebar

away from him in an attempt to swerve, his gut twisting as he realised his mistake.

He cried out, his voice muffled within the confines of the helmet as the shape collided with him.

The handlebars were torn from his grip, and then he was airborne, limp as a rag doll and unable to comprehend what had gone wrong.

The night sky spiralled above him and in the distance, he heard the sickening scrape of metal as his motorbike skidded along the road to a halt.

He screamed as his knees found the asphalt first, the crack of bones inevitable when his body tumbled to the ground.

A moment later, the back of his helmet smacked against the unforgiving hard surface, and darkness claimed him.

TWO

Now

DI Kay Hunter elbowed her way through the door to the incident room of Maidstone police station and bit back a sigh of relief as PC Debbie West reached out for the pile of folders she'd been trying to balance under her arm.

'You shouldn't be carrying these, they weigh a ton,' she scolded. 'You're supposed to be on light duties for at least another eight weeks.'

'Thanks, Debs.' She followed the uniformed officer as she weaved between desks and headed towards the office in the corner of the incident room. 'I thought I'd be okay with those, to be honest. Actually, could you put them on my usual desk?'

Debbie glanced over her shoulder and smiled as she altered course. 'Still not going to use your office?'

Kay grimaced. 'Seems disrespectful, to be honest. I keep thinking Sharp's going to walk through the door any minute and kick me out.'

Debbie dropped the folders onto the desk and waited until Kay sat down. 'Any news?'

'No, but you know as well as I do that Professional Standards investigations are always hush-hush. I guess we won't know the outcome until he does.'

'I still say it's unfair.'

'Yeah, me too, Debs.'

Kay waited until the uniformed officer had wandered back to her own desk, then contemplated the pile of documents strewn in front of her and resisted the urge to groan.

Her injuries at the hands of one of the most diabolical people smugglers the country had ever witnessed had taken longer than anticipated to heal, despite hours of physiotherapy and enforced rest.

The nightmares returned on a regular basis, but she and her other half, Adam, had elected to keep that news to themselves. She was determined that Jozef Demiri wouldn't rule her life after his death – not after what he'd put her and other women through when he was alive.

She'd finally returned to work the previous week, having convinced the occupational health therapist that she was likely to commit a serious crime herself if she had to spend another month cooped up at home.

A compromise had been struck, and she was now relegated to what the police service referred to as "light duties", but which meant she was deskbound for the foreseeable future.

In addition, DCI Angus Larch had stated outright upon her return to work that he expected her to follow orders, and reminded her that her promotion to DI was a probationary one.

Her role to date had resulted in nothing more than a paper-pushing exercise, and she was becoming restless, as well as having a sneaking suspicion that the next few weeks would test her diplomacy skills and patience to the limit.

As it was, she'd spent most of the morning in a training session at headquarters over on Sutton Road, only to be whisked into a management briefing after lunch, and was relieved to return to the incident room at Maidstone police station.

She glanced up as a large mug of tea and a hefty chunk of carrot cake was shoved in front of her, and smiled.

'Thanks, Carys.'

'How're you feeling?'

'Okay. D'you want to round everyone up and we'll do the afternoon briefing?'

'Sure.'

Kay took a sip of tea and watched as the young detective constable made her way through the incident room, laughing and joking with her colleagues as she passed on the message.

She moved with a determined grace that reflected her ambition to work her way up through the ranks, and as she pushed a strand of black hair behind her ear, Kay relaxed.

The woman's confidence had taken a hit over the winter months after a detective sergeant she'd held in high regard had been found to be involved in a corrupt scheme against DI Devon Sharp and his team, and who was now languishing in an open prison for his role.

It seemed that Carys was starting to put the experience behind her.

The events of the past year had exposed the nefarious activities of a senior officer, DCI Simon

Harrison, whose actions had directly impacted Kay and almost resulted in her death.

The personnel at the county police station would take time to recover from the treachery, she was sure, but the fact that Carys seemed to be healing gave her strength.

Kay shivered and buttoned her jacket, trying to ignore the screech of an electric drill from the corridor beyond.

The police station's temperamental heating system had finally shuddered to a halt three days before she'd returned to work, and a ramshackle team of electricians was still trying to pinpoint the location of the fault in the reverse-cycle air conditioning and fix it before the inhabitants of the building froze to death.

In his usual brusque manner, DC Ian Barnes had corralled the team into buying a set of electric heaters to ward off the cold, but they had little effect in the large space of the incident room.

She hated to think what the electricity bill would look like at the end of the month.

As Kay signalled to the team to join her at the front of the room for the morning briefing, Barnes dragged his chair over to where she stood and sat down with a loud sigh.

'You'd think they'd have sorted it out by now,' he

said. 'What's it been? Five – no, six days? At this rate, we're going to need earplugs, or risk being left deaf by the time they've managed to fix it.'

'I can't hear them over an old detective moaning about it,' said Gavin Piper as he perched on the edge of a desk.

Kay laughed as Barnes scrunched up a sheet of paper and aimed it at the younger DC's head. 'All right, enough. Let's get started, shall we?'

'Sarge – sorry, Inspector,' said Gavin.

She waved her hand at him. 'You know the rules – it's "Kay" around here, unless we're outside.'

He grinned, and Kay noted his summer tan had finally had the decency to fade. 'Still can't get used to it.'

'What's the short name for "Inspector", anyway?' said Barnes, scratching his chin. '"Insp?" "Spector?"'

'Stop it,' said Kay, and wagged her finger at him. She ignored the quirk that began at the side of his mouth, and turned her attention back to Gavin. 'Right – what's happening with that break-in over at Aylesford? Got pretty nasty, didn't it?'

'Yes – a retired couple were up late watching television when the glass in the kitchen door was broken and an intruder got in. Threatened to burn their pet dog over the gas hob if they didn't hand over all their valuables. I'm currently waiting on footage from cameras set up at the end of their driveway by a security company over near Sevenoaks,' said the young DC, and raked his fingers through his spiky blond hair. 'The homeowner had some sort of top of the range system installed three months ago and doesn't have access to the files himself. The contact name I was given was supposed to get it to me by Friday, but apparently someone was off sick. If I don't see anything by five o'clock today, I'll give them another call.'

'Do that,' said Kay, 'and if you need me to weigh in, just ask.'

'Will do, thanks.'

'Is the dog okay?' said Debbie.

'Yes, fine. Seemed it was simply used as a threat, nothing else.'

Kay smiled. She had been tempted to ask the same question, and was glad she wasn't the only one wondering about the dog's fate.

'Carys – what's the latest on the spate of break-ins at the industrial estate in Parkwood?'

'We've got a teenager by the name of Calvin Westford in custody downstairs. First time offender, and scared out of his wits – sounds like he joined in as a dare, and didn't realise his mates were serious about breaking and entering the premises. He's currently with PC Norris providing a list of his accomplices.'

A murmur of congratulations filled the room.

'Nice work, well done.' Kay tossed the whiteboard eraser to Carys, who caught it with ease and made her way to the front of the room before wiping the case from the board.

She returned the eraser to Kay, a smile on her face. 'Thanks, guv.'

Kay watched her return to her chair, Gavin providing a high five to his colleague as she sauntered past, and then turned to the folders she'd brought to the front of the room.

'Okay, tasks for tomorrow – Barnes, this one's for you. Suspected arson attack over at that little Indian takeaway on the Tonbridge Road last night. The fire brigade asked us to provide support, so can you follow up with them in the morning?'

'Will do.'

He rose from his seat to take the folder from her, and then began to flick through the pages.

Half an hour later, Kay had set tasks for each of her team and dismissed them for the afternoon.

She returned to her desk and ignored the ache in her forearm, flexing her fingers to ease a muscle spasm as she wiggled her mouse to wake up her computer.

As the team began to filter out of the room at the end of the afternoon's shift, Kay flopped back into her seat with a sigh and surveyed the reports in the tray.

'If this is what being a detective inspector is like, they can keep it,' she muttered. She looked up as Gavin approached her desk. 'Everything okay?'

'Yes,' he said, and shifted his weight from foot to foot. He glanced over his shoulder. 'I just wondered if you'd spoken to DI Sharp recently, and whether there was any news?'

She shook her head. 'Nothing to report yet.'

She didn't mention that she hadn't spoken to their DI for over six weeks, and a wave of guilt washed over her when she realised she'd been so busy concentrating on getting through her health assessments to get back to work that she hadn't given a thought to Sharp's own predicament.

Gavin cleared his throat. 'Okay. Well – I'll see you tomorrow, Kay.'

She forced a smile. 'Will do.'

She rested her chin in her hand as she watched him wind his way between the desks and out through the door of the incident room, his voice carrying over those of Carys and Barnes as the three of them hurried along the corridor towards the exit.

She tossed the folder she was holding into the tray, and then grabbed her bag from under her desk and checked her watch.

Maybe it was time to catch up with Detective Inspector Devon Sharp, after all.

THREE

'A beard?'

'You don't like it?'

'Well, it's… different.'

Kay managed to stop gaping and made her way over the threshold of DI Devon Sharp's house before he closed the door and waved her towards the kitchen.

Rebecca, Sharp's wife, worked at a local childcare centre and given the sound of rock music from the back of the house, was still at work. The way the childcare centre worked, the management staff took turns either working an early morning or a late afternoon to be present when children were dropped off or collected, in case parents wanted to speak to someone.

Kay didn't know anything about the Sharps' own

children, save for photographs she'd previously seen of a healthy-looking pair of teenaged twins that took pride of place on a bookshelf in the sitting room.

'Cup of tea?'

'Please.'

She shrugged off her wool coat and placed it on the back of one of the stylish chairs that surrounded a matching dining table off to one side of the wide space, and dumped her bag on the surface before wandering across the room and leaning against the sink while Sharp turned down the music blaring from a set of speakers on the windowsill.

'How're you holding up?'

'Like crap, but then you'd know all about that.'

She nodded, but said nothing.

'It's the boredom, Kay.'

He ran a hand over brown hair that now held the faintest traces of silver and had grown longer over the winter months, and then shook his head.

'How's Bec?'

'Stoical. As always.'

Kay smiled.

Sharp's wife was like her own partner, Adam. Dependable, not easily flustered, and completely at a loss as to why her other half would throw himself heart and soul into a career that was at worst ungrateful, and at best trying.

'What about you? Glad to be back at work?'

'I'm bored, Devon. They've got me on light duties.' She lifted her arm. 'I'm taking longer to heal than they thought, and apparently I can't risk overdoing it.'

'Bet that's going down well.'

'Shut up and give me a cup of tea.'

They both laughed.

Kay fell silent as he moved about the kitchen, fetching milk from the refrigerator and fishing the tea bags out of the mug once the drinks had stewed.

He may have been laughing and joking with her, but she could sense the frustration and desperation under the surface of his carefully controlled emotions.

Despite his attempts at normality, the effect of the past three months boiled under the surface.

She knew first-hand how a Professional Standards investigation could prey on an officer's confidence and health, especially if that officer was innocent of any wrongdoing.

'You don't take sugar, do you?'

Kay shook her head to clear her thoughts and tried to refocus. 'No, that's right – thanks.'

'Come on through to the conservatory. Bec's got

me painting the windowsills, so I can work while we chat and I won't get into trouble for slacking in my duties.'

He winked, then led the way across the room and through an archway to a wide enclosed space that overlooked a garden.

Kay squinted through the window and cast her gaze over the twilight-heavy patio and lawn.

Sharp's house was in an estate on the opposite side of Maidstone to hers, but the main road that cut through the scattered cul-de-sacs soon turned to country lane as it wound its way out to the village of Otham, and she knew he often saw foxes pass through his garden.

The garden was silent for now, though, and she turned back to the room to see him eyeing her warily over his mug of tea, the paint brushes ignored.

She placed her drink on the small table next to one of the wicker armchairs and dropped the pretence.

'Devon, I need something to get my teeth into before I go crazy. This whole thing about being a DI – after what I could see happening politically last year, I never wanted to be a part of that. I love being a detective. All I've done this past week is shuffle paperwork.'

He shrugged. 'Sometimes, that's all there is –

making sure the manpower is spread evenly around the area. It's still important.'

'But it's not *doing*, is it?'

'So, Demiri didn't put you off being on the frontline?'

She shook her head. 'If anything, it's made me more determined to put people like him away – before they ever get a chance to do what he did.'

His eyes narrowed. 'What do you want from me?'

Kay crossed her arms. 'I want to know why there's a Professional Standards investigation against you, and I want to know what I can do to help.'

He chuckled, and gestured to the two armchairs. 'Is this simply a ruse to get me back, so I can take care of the paperwork?'

She held up her hand as she sat. 'All right, so I might have an ulterior motive.'

He placed his mug on the coffee table between them, and then leaned back in his chair with a sigh.

'The problem is, Kay, if you try to help me, you might damage your own chances of advancement within the force.'

'Even more than I did last year?'

His eyes hardened. 'Don't joke about it, Kay. You fought hard to clear your name and see justice served last year, and it very nearly killed you. Don't throw that away.'

She took a sip of tea to digest his words, and then set her mug down next to his. 'And yet, you did the same for me. We're a team, Devon. We have been for a long time. Let me help you.'

'You have to promise to be careful, Kay. If you're going to do this, do it by the book. Remember, it's all about the politics and that means you're going to have to work with Larch at some point.'

She grimaced, then conceded the point. 'All right.'

He nodded, and picked up his tea once more. 'Where do you want to start?'

'What happened between you and DCI Simon Harrison?'

FOUR

'Harrison was the investigating officer in a case involving the death of a young motorcyclist on the A20 between Leeds and Harrietsham, and already had a reputation for cutting corners to manage his caseload.'

Kay shuffled forward on her chair and rested her elbows on her knees. 'When was this?'

'Ten years ago.'

'You weren't with the Kent Police at the time.'

'No, I was still in the military police, and you know what everyone thinks of them.'

She managed a smile. The military police had its own way of dealing with its investigations, and wasn't always well respected amongst her colleagues for doing so. 'Go on.'

'Because the accident happened off barracks, Kent Police were in attendance. I could only be an observer.'

'What happened?'

'A young recruit by the name of Jamie Ingram was killed one night in December. It was raining, the conditions were less than ideal, and it was late. The driver of an articulated truck came across the scene only moments after it had happened – the engine of the bike was still warm.'

Kay pulled out her phone and selected the "maps" app. 'Whereabouts on that stretch of road?'

'Just before the Broomfield turnoff.'

She ran her eyes over the map before her, and frowned. 'Strange place to lose control, especially given that the bends there were straightened out over thirty years ago. Was there oil on the surface, or was he going too fast for the conditions?'

She put her phone away, then lifted her gaze to Sharp.

He was glaring at her.

'What?'

'Jamie Ingram was one of the best motorcyclists I've ever known. I went to school with his father, who still owns the farm Jamie grew up on. By the time he was nine years old, Jamie had a small motorbike and used to go tearing around one of the fields his dad had set aside especially for that purpose. He was winning motocross competitions two years later at a national level.'

'So, he could handle a bike in any condition, is that what you're saying?'

Sharp's features softened. 'Yes. That's exactly what I'm saying.' He pushed himself out of his chair and shoved his hands in his jeans pockets as he paced the floor. 'Sorry. It's just that at the time – and now – I want to do what's right for Jamie and his parents.'

'We were talking about the road conditions that night.'

'The lead investigator concluded there was no oil on the road, and there was no sign of any other debris that might have caused Jamie to lose control.'

'Wildlife?'

'The verges were checked, but they found no injured rabbits, and a deer would have made a hell of an impact on the motorbike. There was nothing like that.'

'What was the investigator's conclusion?'

'His report stated that, for whatever reason, Jamie made a sudden deviation to his line taking the corner and lost control.'

Kay leaned back in her chair and rubbed the base

of her skull before dropping her phone back into her bag. 'I'm getting a crick in my neck.'

Sharp took the hint and sat down with a loud sigh.

'And what do you think happened, Devon?'

'I spoke to his commanding officer the day after the accident. Apparently, Jamie had phoned the adjutant the previous morning, requesting an urgent meeting with Lieutenant Colonel Stephen Carterton. The only appointment available was for the Thursday afternoon—'

'And Jamie died before he could speak to him.'

'Yes.'

'Any idea what Jamie wanted to talk to him about?'

'No, but that's not the point. It's highly unusual for a private to make a request like that. Something must've been worrying Jamie to make that appointment in the first place, let alone phone it in while he was off barracks.'

'What do the family think?'

Sharp scratched at his beard. 'At the time, his father raised concerns that Jamie was nervous when he returned home from Afghanistan.'

'Post-traumatic stress disorder?'

'No – Jamie hadn't been exposed to anything that could have triggered that; he was involved in supplies and logistics and the like. He wouldn't talk about it to his parents when asked, but they said when Jamie's mobile phone rang that night, he'd started shaking and had taken the call outside. He wouldn't tell them what it was about. That was the night of his death.'

'I don't get it. Why would there be a PS investigation into your conduct based on this?'

Sharp shrugged. 'An accusation has been made by a senior officer against me – Harrison. He's trying to suggest that I didn't report all the facts to him ten years ago, when I did, and that I may have *somehow* been involved in what happened to Jamie and tried to cover it up. It's all bullshit, of course. I suppose until they've got through the investigation into his activities, they're holding judgement on whether to suspend me indefinitely, or drop the PS case and let me get back to work.' He gestured to the discarded paint brushes. 'In the meantime, I sit around and wait.'

'All right. What do *you* think happened ten years ago?'

Sharp twisted in his chair at the sound of the front door opening, then turned back to Kay and lowered his voice. 'I think Jamie found out something was going on within his regiment, and intended to report it. I think he was killed before he got a chance to do so.'

Kay felt the air leave her lungs as Rebecca Sharp appeared at the archway leading through to the conservatory, and plastered a smile on her face to hide her shock at her colleague's statement.

'Kay – how lovely to see you.'

Kay stood and accepted the other woman's quick hug. 'How're you doing, Bec?'

'Oh, you know. Running out of jobs for Devon. The sooner he's back at work, the better.' Her brow creased. 'Is that why you're here?'

Kay caught the look Sharp shot her, and shook her head. 'No, unfortunately I don't have any news about that. I only got back to work myself last week, and I've spent the past six days feeling like I'm pedalling backwards.'

Bec chuckled. 'Yeah, that's what promotion will do to you.'

'I should let you two get on,' said Kay, and plucked her bag from the tiled floor. 'Great to see you, Bec.'

'You too, Kay.'

Sharp followed her out to the front door, then unlocked it and stood to one side before handing Kay a piece of paper.

'Here. This is the address for Jamie Ingram's family. Speak to them. Get a feel for what Jamie was like as a person. Then you'll understand.'

'So, we're doing this, are we?'

'Up for it?'

'You bet.'

He smiled. 'By the way, how's Adam doing?'

Kay checked her watch. 'Oh, bloody hell.'

'What's wrong?'

'It's his birthday today, and right now I'm late taking him out to dinner.'

FIVE

Kay pushed through the front door to her house and shrugged her coat off her shoulders before hanging it over the newel post.

'Sorry I'm late!'

'Up here.'

She ran up the stairs two at a time and made her way to the master bedroom, dumping her bag on the bed as her other half, Adam Turner, emerged from the en suite in a cloud of steam.

'What time's the table booked for?'

He grinned. 'It *was* booked for six-thirty, but I guessed you were running late, so I've asked them to change it to half seven.'

'You're a star.' She kissed him, and then

unbuttoned her blouse and tossed it into the laundry basket next to the door.

As she flicked through the clothes hanging in her wardrobe trying to decide what to wear, her heartbeat began to settle. She hated that her job encroached on her home life sometimes, but especially when it was Adam's birthday and they'd arranged to treat themselves to a meal at an expensive restaurant they favoured for special occasions.

'Do you want me to order a taxi?' said Adam. He pushed a cufflink through the sleeve of his shirt and buttoned it.

'That's okay – I was going to offer to drive. I've got an early start tomorrow, so I can only have one drink anyway.'

He reached out and slapped her bum before dodging out of the way as she spun around. Grinning, he moved to the door.

'Take your time. I'll see you downstairs.'

Kay smiled and turned her attention back to the wardrobe before selecting a black dress with spaghetti straps and a red shawl to cover her shoulders.

The stately home that housed the restaurant was beautiful, but could be draughty in the late winter months.

Adam's voice filtered through the floorboards

from the kitchen, and she realised that he'd brought home a patient. By the sounds of it, whatever it was had been let out into the garden before they went out to dinner and was now being resettled for the evening.

Smiling, and with a little trepidation as to what she'd find in her house this time, she finished dressing and then grabbed a small handbag and her shoes and padded downstairs.

A large Alsatian dog eased itself from its bed on the tiles as she entered the kitchen, its brown eyes doleful as it padded across to her and nuzzled her hand.

Adam leaned against the kitchen worktop, a glass of water in his hand. 'Meet Rufus. He used to be a service dog with Kent Police, but was fostered out about four years ago. His foster family are away at the moment, so I've agreed to babysit.'

'Hello, Rufus.'

The dog snorted, and then turned back to the old duvet Adam had folded up and placed in one corner as a makeshift bed before curling up on it with a groan.

'What's wrong with him?'

Adam sighed and put his glass down. 'Terminal cancer, unfortunately. We've tried everything over the past six months, but it's not working and it's not fair to keep treating him with stuff that isn't working.'

Kay lowered her voice, a lump forming in her throat. 'Will you have to put him to sleep?'

'Not yet. He's responding well to the painkillers at the moment, and he seems to be getting around on his own okay – he hasn't lost his appetite, either. I'll continue to monitor him, obviously, and I'll be having a chat with the foster family when they get back from Wales to discuss their options.'

Kay picked up her car keys while she contemplated the man in front of her.

One of the town's busiest and well-respected veterinarians, he was also one of the most compassionate people she knew. Rufus was in good hands, that much was certain.

'When are his foster family back?'

'About ten days, I think. Graham's mother-in-law died yesterday, and I'd imagine by the time they get all the paperwork sorted out and the funeral arranged it'll be at least that.' He checked his watch. 'We'd better get a move on if we're going to make that reservation.'

Thirty minutes later, the car's tyres were crackling over the gravel apron that stretched around the stately home in the middle of the Kentish countryside, and then Kay put her arm through Adam's as they walked towards the stone steps leading into the seventeenth-century manor house that was now a hotel and restaurant.

A smartly dressed member of staff held open the door for them, and Kay let her shoulders relax as they were shown to their table.

The luxurious surroundings of the dining room cocooned them from the outside world. Floor-to-ceiling curtains covered the windows, and the thick carpet softened the noise from other tables as they passed.

The clink of cutlery and muted conversations reached her ears, and her mouth watered at the thought of savouring the food.

Pleased to find they had been given a table in the far corner away from other diners, she smiled as the waiter pulled out her chair for her and fussed around them pouring water and taking their order.

She waited until he had returned with their wine and moved across the room to another table, before she clinked her glass against Adam's.

'Happy birthday.'

'Thank you.'

Kay took a sip of her wine before placing it on the linen tablecloth.

'So, tell me more about Rufus. He seems friendly. I always thought you had to be careful around ex-service dogs.'

'He's too old now, I think. Perhaps he realises he's not got long, so he's making the most of it. The foster family have a young daughter, and Graham says they've never had any issues. Rufus is very protective of her.'

'It'll be nice having him around. We haven't had any of your guests for a while.'

'And none as highly commended as Rufus – he was quite the police dog in his day.'

Kay had to put down her wine glass as Adam regaled her with some of the dog's exploits as a serving officer with Kent Police, fearing she'd splutter out her drink over the table.

By the time their main courses were served, her sides were aching. She held up her hand.

'Okay, enough. I'm hurting.'

Adam winked, then tucked into the juicy steak that had been set in front of him.

They fell to silence for a while, enjoying the food and fine wine, until Kay put down her utensils and cleared her throat.

'I want to help Sharp, Adam.'

'Bored already?'

She glanced up, but he was wearing a broad smile. 'Is it that obvious?'

'Are you kidding me? I knew the moment you walked back through the door to that incident room you were going to be looking for an opportunity to get your sleeves rolled up. I'm surprised it's taken you until now.'

'How long were you going to go without mentioning it?'

His mouth quirked. 'I'd have held out longer than you.'

She moved to slap his arm playfully, but he moved too quickly and laughed.

'Just stay out of trouble this time, Hunter.'

SIX

Kay waited until after the morning briefing before returning to her desk and logging into the HOLMES database.

As she waited for the computer to retrieve the information about the death of Jamie Ingram, she nibbled the ragged edge of her thumbnail and tried to strategize for the days ahead.

First, she had to get herself up to speed on the original investigation managed by Simon Harrison, a detective constable at the time.

Second, she wanted to head out to the site of Jamie's fatal accident – it was all very well reading through reports and the like, but she knew she'd get a better understanding of the circumstances if she did so.

And she had to speak with Jamie's parents.

The screen in front of her blinked, and then a set of search results were displayed.

Kay scanned the information before clicking on the only subject heading that contained all the keywords she'd entered.

A second screen loaded, and she began to scroll through the potted information from Simon Harrison's investigation into the motorcycle accident.

Having worked with the man before, she felt it was evident that his gung-ho attitude to solving cases was already well formed when he'd become a detective constable.

His note-taking was sparse, and it seemed that he'd had the view that Jamie was simply a motorcyclist who knew the risks, but took them anyway.

The enquiry database provided a series of links to three traffic infringements for speeding, and Kay noted that at the time of his death, Jamie had only three points left on his licence.

She cupped her chin in her hand and sighed while she leafed through the pages and a photocopy of a road map depicting the A20 route from the Ingrams' farm to Broomfield in the folder before her.

'What are you working on, guv?'

Gavin's voice jerked her from her reverie, and she shoved the map across her desk away from him.

'Just some historical stuff.'

'Did you go and see Sharp last night?'

'Yeah.'

'How is he?'

'Anxious. Bored.'

'Anything we can do to help?'

Carys had wandered over, and now perched on Barnes's desk opposite Kay's.

Kay sighed. She'd worked with the small team for over a year now, and it seemed they knew her better than she'd realised. She waved a hand at the folder from archives, and then at her computer screen.

'I haven't got all the details, but you can bet it's a last-ditch attempt by Harrison to discredit him. The Professional Standards investigation stemmed from an accusation made by Harrison. He made claims about Sharp's actions in an older case from ten years ago after Sharp reported Harrison's activities late last year as gross misconduct.'

'When Harrison used you as bait to draw out Jozef Demiri, you mean?' said Barnes. He rested his elbows on his desk. 'Go on.'

'Well, when I asked him about it Sharp said that when he was still serving in the military police, a young army recruit was killed in a motorbike accident on the A20 between Leeds and Harrietsham. Because it happened off barracks, Kent Police were involved. Harrison was stationed at Maidstone back then, and was the investigating officer. Harrison now claims Sharp withheld evidence to protect the army's reputation, whereas Sharp felt that the original investigation wasn't carried out properly by Harrison, and voiced his concerns at the time.'

'And we all know about Harrison's reputation for doing anything to get a result,' said Gavin.

Kay noticed how he ran a hand over his misshapen nose. 'Exactly.'

'So, Harrison cut corners to get a quick result back then, you mean?' said Carys.

'Yeah. The general consensus was that it was an accidental death caused by misadventure, and that was supported by the coroner's inquest. Sharp maintained at the time, and still does, that there was more to it.'

'Why has Sharp been placed under a Professional Standards investigation for it?' said Gavin.

'Because of what happened last year, I guess the powers that be need to make sure the antagonism between Sharp and Harrison didn't affect the outcome of this case.'

'Well, there's no love lost between the RMPs and the police,' said Barnes, his mouth twitching. 'What's all this got to do with you?'

Kay shrugged. 'I've known Sharp for a long time. If he thinks there's more to Jamie Ingram's demise than a case of accidental death, then I'm inclined to trust his instincts.'

Barnes pushed himself out of his chair, leaned across, and plucked one of the documents from Kay's desk. He raised an eyebrow.

'It says here that Sharp is a friend of the Ingram family. Don't you think that may have influenced his thinking?'

'Maybe, but I won't find out until I've taken a closer look and spoken to them.'

'Any reason why you're keeping this to yourself?' said Carys. She folded her arms.

Kay glanced from her to the other two detectives standing around her desk. 'Well, I just thought it'd probably be safer to leave you lot out of it. You've got promising careers ahead of you, after all.' Her mouth quirked. 'Apart from Barnes, of course.'

'Oi.'

She waited until the laughter had subsided, then grew serious once more. 'Look, according to Sharp, this might uncover some stuff that could make things difficult around here politically. After all, the whole Division is under a cloud thanks to Harrison's actions last year, despite the result we got. I didn't want to drag you all into it with me. Not like last time.'

Barnes snorted. 'You've never made any of us do anything we didn't want to do, Kay. We've always been a team. That means we look out for Sharp, too. He'd do the same for any of us. He stood up for you.'

Kay peered around his shoulder and made sure the other officers working at the far end of the incident room were out of earshot.

'We need to keep it between us until I can convince DCI Larch we have grounds to reopen a cold case and we've gathered enough evidence to prove Sharp's theory, is that understood?'

'Understood,' said Gavin. He drew closer and then leaned down and removed the road map from Kay's desk before casting his eyes over the demarcated crash site. 'Anything to help Sharp, right?'

'Are you absolutely sure you want to do this?'

Gavin and Carys nodded, their faces eager.

'All for one,' said Barnes.

SEVEN

Kay had noticed on her return to work that the DCI she'd known the previous year had changed dramatically in her absence.

Gone was the forthright, obnoxious senior officer she'd crossed swords with more than once. In his place was a man who, frankly, appeared shrunken, and she wondered what impact the past three months had had on him.

Despite his outward appearances, it must've been devastating for him to have one detective in hospital and another more senior and well-respected detective under the shadow of an internal investigation, despite the closure of one of Kent's biggest people smuggling organisations in history.

Where once Angus Larch could be counted upon

to create problems for her, in his place was a man who seemed reticent – even cowed.

She hadn't yet gained the measure of the reasons, either. Being away from the hustle and bustle of the county town's police station had sheltered her from the political fallout of the previous case she and Sharp had worked on, and she felt that she was still finding her feet in her new role despite the confidence she made sure shone through.

She shuffled in her seat, and placed the manila folder on her lap while the DCI took his place behind his desk and clasped his hands in front of him.

'You and I normally go out of our way to avoid each other, Hunter, so what on earth would bring you to my door on a wet windy morning?'

'I think I've got a way for us to improve our targets, guv.'

'All right. You've got my attention.'

Kay had spent the previous night at home strategizing her approach to her senior officer. She knew she had to play to his ego and that of the Division, and so she wasn't overly concerned by the impromptu meeting. In fact, she was looking forward to the challenge.

'Sir, I believe I've enough evidence to suggest that we reopen the case in the death of Jamie Ingram.'

She watched as Larch's eyes narrowed.

'Motorcycle accident, wasn't it? About ten years ago?'

'That's the one.'

He unclasped his hands and leaned back in his chair. 'Go on.'

'At the time, the investigating officer neglected to take into account the victim's experience as a motorcyclist. He also failed to account for evidence from the Royal Military Police to the effect that the victim had arranged an urgent meeting with his commanding officer – one that he never attended, due to his death occurring some two days prior to that meeting.'

When Larch remained silent, she continued.

'Ingram had received a phone call the night of his death. At the time, his parents stated that he appeared extremely nervous upon returning from his last posting. He wouldn't tell them anything when questioned. According to witnesses, it's very unusual for a private to request a meeting with his commanding officer, too. Something must've been bothering him.'

Larch clicked his fingers and motioned to the folder in Kay's lap. 'Your notes?'

'Guv.'

She passed the folder across the desk to him, and crossed her legs.

'Harrison was the investigating officer, wasn't he?'

'Yes, guv. Working out of Maidstone at the time, prior to transferring to the Met.'

'What was the military police conclusion in the case?'

'The official line was that there wasn't enough evidence to suggest foul play.'

'And Sharp was the army liaison?'

'Yes.'

He flicked through the pages before raising his gaze to hers. 'Have you spoken to Sharp?'

'Yes, guv.'

'How is he?'

'Frustrated, guv.'

'Hmm.'

She waited while he read the one-page executive summary she'd prepared and left on the top of the documents in the file, before he began to delve into the contents of the folder once more. After what seemed an age, she could bear the silence no longer.

'Guv, I've been thinking that given Harrison's reputation for shoddy investigative work, evidenced by his actions late last year, and that Sharp is currently under a Professional Standards investigation instigated by Harrison, we should take another look into Jamie Ingram's death. Perhaps Sharp was right at the time. Maybe there was more to this than was uncovered by Harrison.'

Larch dropped the folder onto the desk between them and folded his arms across his chest. 'What's your motive, Hunter?'

'Motive, guv?'

'Why are you getting involved?'

Kay lowered her gaze, and then raised her head once more and met his eyes. 'I owe him, guv. We were a good team, and it's not fair what's happened to him. Just because Harrison's been caught out, it doesn't mean it's right to fling mud at Sharp. He's one of the best we've got.'

He ran a hand over his jaw, then leaned forward. 'The PS investigation into Sharp's conduct was a political move by East Division. Sort of a tit-for-tat over our exposure of Harrison. We got burned thanks to DS O'Reilly's involvement with Harrison last year, but not as badly as them. At the moment, the powers that be are looking at how the next year's budget will be apportioned through the county.'

'So, it'd be in our interest to prove Sharp was right about the Ingram death. After all, if he's right, and Harrison got it wrong, then we have a murderer who's been walking around free for the past ten years, haven't we? And, if we solve this, it'd help to put the pressure on East Division. Great media exposure for West Division, right?'

'You know, for someone who professes not to be interested in the politics of the role, Hunter, you certainly have a keen sense of playing the game.'

Kay swallowed, lost for words. 'I– I—'

He smiled; something that she'd never seen DCI Angus Larch do in her presence.

She was reminded of a shark.

He stabbed his forefinger on the folder. 'How sure are you about this?'

She took a deep breath and spent the next five minutes running through the known facts from the original investigation and her intended course of action, and then sat back in her seat and waited.

Larch spun back and forth in his chair, staring at the ceiling while he contemplated her words. Finally, he lowered his gaze to hers and sat forwards.

'All right. I agree you have enough grounds to reopen the case. What are you going to do about resources?'

'I've spoken to Detectives Barnes, Miles, and Piper,' said Kay. 'They're all keen to be a part of the investigation, and given their current caseload, I believe this would take no more than one to two hours a day within current parameters.'

'So, no additional budget requirements?'

'No, guv.'

She didn't mention that the team had already agreed to work out of hours if it would prove Sharp's assertion that Jamie Ingram's death wasn't an accident.

They would do everything it took to get Sharp back to work.

'All right.' He pushed the folder towards her. 'Consider my approval given.'

Kay rose from her chair and tucked the folder under her arm. 'That's great, guv. Thanks.'

He nodded.

She turned away from his desk, but then paused and glanced over her shoulder. 'Guv? I know we haven't always seen eye to eye, but—'

She paused, unsure how to continue.

Larch raised an eyebrow. 'Spit it out, Hunter.'

'You look tired, guv. Is everything all right?'

He snorted. 'Apart from having you back here, nagging me to get you off light duties, you mean?'

She forced a smile, but said nothing.

He sighed, and waved her away. 'Nothing to

concern yourself with at the moment, Hunter. Now, get out of my hair and don't let me catch you stirring up trouble like you usually do.'

She moved to the door, and turned at the last minute.

'We're all on the same side, guv. Remember that.'

EIGHT

Four expectant faces turned to her as she entered the incident room at six o'clock that evening.

'Debbie? What are you still doing here?'

'You need all the help you can get,' said the uniformed police constable. 'And I want to help.'

'Thank you.'

'What did Larch have to say?' said Barnes, turning in his chair as Kay strode past and headed for Sharp's office.

'We're on.'

'*Yes.*' Gavin high-fived Carys.

'Come on. In here.'

'Thought you weren't going to use Sharp's office?' said Carys.

Kay waited until the four of them had joined her.

'This way, we keep our investigation separate from the day-to-day running of the incident room,' she said. 'Although Larch has approved the investigation, politically I think he's nervous that East Division will find out – they're still smarting about us exposing Harrison last year.'

'Tit for tat,' said Barnes.

'That's exactly what he said. There's no overtime available either, so if you have second thoughts, tell me. It's not a problem – you all have lives outside of work and other responsibilities.'

She motioned to Barnes to help her, and then pulled a spare whiteboard from the incident room into Sharp's office and placed it against the wall, pushing his desk to one side to make room for it.

Gavin moved a threadbare visitor's chair across to the window while Carys and Debbie brought in spares, and then Kay opened her folder and pinned a photograph of Jamie Ingram to the whiteboard.

'A quick recap of some of the information you haven't heard yet,' she said. 'Jamie Ingram was killed in a motorcycle accident ten years ago. It occurred on the A20 between Leeds and Hollingbourne, close to the T-junction for Broomfield. Like I said, at the time, the Kent Police investigation was overseen by Simon Harrison.'

A murmur of discontent mumbled around the room, and she saw Barnes's top lip curl upwards in a sneer.

'Yes, I know what you all think of him, but let me continue. Sharp was still in the army at the time, in the Royal Military Police. The army couldn't claim jurisdiction on the investigation because it happened off barracks, but Sharp knew Jamie's parents, and undertook his own investigation in tandem with that of Kent Police. I believe that's where the antagonism between Sharp and Harrison arises from. Harrison already had a reputation then for doing anything to close a case, and Sharp had raised concerns that there may be more to Jamie's accident than was originally established.'

'What happened when the coroner's inquest ruled it as an accident?' said Carys. 'What did the army have to say about it?'

'The army accepted the ruling. I get the impression from reading through the original file that they thought Sharp's insistence that foul play was involved was a bit of a stretch.'

'What do we know about Jamie Ingram?' said Barnes.

'A model soldier, by the sounds of it. No disciplinary record, no problems when he was off barracks. Apart from a couple of speeding fines, he didn't cause any trouble as far as I can tell. So, why was he killed?'

'Reasons for motive,' said Gavin, counting off his fingers. 'Revenge, money, jealousy—'

'All right, Mister passed-his-exam-last-year,' said Barnes. 'Now narrow it down and tell us why.'

'You say Sharp mentioned that Jamie made an appointment with his commanding officer prior to dying,' said Carys. 'What if someone had something to hide, found out Jamie was about to blow the whistle about it, and decided to kill him?'

'All right. What?'

'Must've been something big, to want to silence him permanently,' said Barnes.

'Sharp said that Jamie's father stated that his son received a phone call the night of his death, and seemed shaken by it. He couldn't hear what was being said, because Jamie took one look at the number and disappeared outside to answer the phone,' said Kay. She scribbled in her notebook. 'I'll ask the parents if Jamie's mobile phone was returned to them after the inquest.'

'Do you think they'd have kept it all this time?' said Gavin.

'You'd be surprised at what grieving families hold

on to. Especially mobile phones – often the voicemail message on it is the last time they'll hear that person's voice.'

'I'll go through the database and see if anything was retained at headquarters,' said Debbie.

'Thanks – that's one thing off my list. Okay, tasks for tomorrow then. Carys, can you track down the original senior investigating officer from Traffic? Harrison wouldn't have been given that role, but would've liaised with that person. Please set up a time for me to meet him or her at the original crash site, as I'd like to see it for myself.'

'Will do.'

'Barnes, I plan to visit Jamie Ingram's parents tomorrow. I'd like you to come with me, so we'll introduce ourselves officially and let them know we're reopening the investigation. You'll be my deputy on this one, all right?'

'Sounds good.'

'Gavin, can you go through the original statements with Debbie and let me know if we need to go back and clarify anything? I'd also like a list drawn up of people we ought to speak to again, especially his colleagues in the army. Find out where his commanding officer is these days – I want to speak to him this week, if possible.'

'Guv.' He gave her a lopsided grin as she opened her mouth to correct him. 'Yeah, yeah – I know.'

They all laughed.

Kay rubbed at her right eye. 'All right, that's enough for today. All this has to be done after your usual day-to-day tasks. We can't let our usual commitments slip, is that understood?'

A murmur of agreement echoed off the walls of the office.

'Okay, see you in the morning. Let's see if Sharp is onto something.'

NINE

'I'm presuming by the way you bounced through the front door, that Larch has given you the go-ahead.'

Kay grinned as she placed her handbag on the kitchen worktop and ruffled the fur between Rufus's ears.

'You got it.'

Adam handed her a glass of wine as she eased herself onto one of the barstools and kicked off her shoes. He gestured to her arm.

'Are you going to be okay running that investigation on top of everything else you have to do? After all, you've only just finished physiotherapy.'

'I'll be fine. If the past week is anything to go by, I spent most of my time delegating work to everybody else while I have to sit in meetings at headquarters.'

'Will you still have to go to those?'

She wrinkled her nose. 'Probably.'

'It's a shame you can't delegate those to someone.'

She turned her attention to the dog at her side. 'How has this one been today?'

Adam shrugged. 'Grumbling a bit. I'm keeping an eye on him. Like people when they're ill, he has his good days and bad. Don't worry – he's only been on the low dose of painkillers so far, and I've increased those a little. He's still eating, and he loves going out in the garden during the day.'

Kay sipped her wine and rubbed the back of her neck. A satisfying *click* reached her ears as a muscle eased loose, and she closed her eyes.

'I heard that,' said Adam. 'You're too tense.'

She opened her eyes and smiled. 'I was too tense sitting around doing nothing. It's much better having something to focus on, and best of all the others are all interested in helping, too.'

'How is that going to work?'

'Well, Larch has made it quite clear I have to manage this on my own time. Gavin caught me looking through the old files, and before I knew it they all wanted in on the investigation. They're doing a lot of the legwork for me in between their other work commitments, and we can have a briefing every evening to keep track of progress. We all miss Sharp, Adam. We want him back.'

Adam's response was interrupted by the doorbell.

'I'll get it – it'll be Deepak with the food.'

Kay waited while Adam padded out to the front door and chatted with the elderly man whose family ran their favourite Indian takeaway.

The man left his nephews to manage the business, preferring to run the delivery side of it instead and catch up with regular customers such as Kay and Adam who relied on the local takeout service when they were too busy – or too tired – to cook for themselves.

She could hear Adam joking with him now as he handed over the cash for the meal before the front door closed, and the sound of Adam's footsteps reached her ears.

She glanced up as he re-entered the kitchen, and then raised an eyebrow. 'Three portions?'

He managed to look a little contrite. 'I got Rufus a chicken biryani.'

'Is that wise?'

Adam's eyes fell to the Alsatian who had raised

his head from the duvet in the corner. 'It's okay, I asked them to avoid onions or anything that dogs shouldn't eat and it's not very spicy. I figured he deserves it. He's on borrowed time, after all. He might as well enjoy himself.'

Kay smiled as Adam placed the carry bag on the worktop beside her, fetched plates from the cupboard above the microwave and then dished up their food before taking half of the contents from the third container and shovelling it into Rufus's bowl.

He ruffled the dog's ears as he placed the bowl next to the folded duvet, then grinned as Rufus buried his snout in the rice.

'I think he's inhaling that,' said Kay, and topped up their wine glasses.

'Told you he'd like it.'

They fell silent for a while, each savouring the spices and flavours of their favourite dishes before Kay put down her fork and took a sip of her wine.

'God, that's delicious. I hope they never sell the business.'

'I know.' Adam pushed away his empty plate and eased back onto his bar stool, a look of contentment on his face. 'What are the next steps with your investigation?'

'Barnes and I are going to head out to the

Ingrams' farm tomorrow lunchtime to speak with Jamie's parents. We need to let them know the case is being reopened as a courtesy anyway, plus I want to review their statements with them from ten years ago and see if I can uncover anything that Harrison didn't consider.'

'Larch is okay with you doing this?'

'Yes – in fact, he seemed quite supportive. I think I convinced him that the risk of reopening a case that had been previously closed by Harrison in a rush might serve him well if we can prove Sharp's theory.'

'By making Larch look good, you mean?'

'Yeah.'

Adam picked up his wine glass and tilted it against hers. He winked. 'Becoming quite the politician, Hunter.'

Kay jutted out her chin and set her glass down. 'Don't you start. That's what he said.'

Adam laughed. 'Don't take it the wrong way. It's good – it means you're learning to use their ambitions to suit your own needs. You get Sharp back if this all goes to plan, right?'

She smiled, and then sighed. 'Yeah, you're right. I miss having him around.'

He grew serious. 'You really don't like the promotion, do you?'

'Not if it's going to be like it has been for the past week, no. I don't want to be stuck in an office sending everyone else out to do the interesting stuff. I'm used to rolling up my sleeves and getting stuck in.'

'How will they take it if you resign the role and go back to being a detective sergeant, do you think?'

She shrugged. 'I doubt they'll ask me again.'

'Do you mind that?'

'I don't know.'

'Well,' he said, gathering their plates and taking them over to the sink. 'Perhaps get this case out of the way and see how you feel. Don't act too hastily though, okay? I wouldn't want you to regret anything.'

TEN

Kay scrolled through another batch of newly arrived emails on her phone as Barnes navigated the pool car along winding narrow bends towards the Ingrams' farm.

She sighed before tossing the phone back into her bag at her feet, then turned her attention to the passing countryside as the windscreen wipers drummed an intermittent beat.

High hedgerows on each side of the lane hid fields from view but, every once in a while, the car passed a gap caused by a gate, and a glimpse of barren land flashed past in an instant, the skeletal remains of trees stark against the grey sky.

'At least it's not raining hard,' said Barnes. 'I

don't fancy walking across a bloody farmyard in this weather as it is.'

Kay turned away from the window and peered at his foot on the accelerator.

'Blimey, I'm not surprised, wearing those shoes.'

His mouth thinned. 'Emma insisted I buy them. Says they're more fitting for a detective than my usual pair. She's become rather opinionated since starting university.'

'Is that so?'

'She bought them for my birthday last month, so I couldn't say "no", could I?'

'And what do you think of them?'

'My feet are killing me.'

Kay laughed, then pointed to a signpost they were approaching.

'This is the place. The farm should be a mile or so up here.'

'I read the statement Harrison took from Jamie's father ten years ago,' said Barnes, flicking on the indicator and braking before turning left. 'I didn't realise Sharp served with him in the army.'

'Yeah – joined up at the same time, apparently. Michael Ingram was demobbed after three years when his father died suddenly, and he took over the running of the family farm instead.'

Barnes slowed as a low barn structure came into view over the top of a hedge. 'How do you want to do this?'

'I've been thinking about that. I'd like to start off by explaining that the investigation into Jamie's death has been reopened, and then let them tell us what happened at the time, rather than reviewing the old statements they gave.'

'You think the past ten years might've uncovered some more information?'

'Perhaps. I'm sure they've gone over and over in their minds what happened.'

'I didn't get the impression from their original statements that they thought foul play was involved.'

'No, but I think Sharp and Jamie's father kept that theory to themselves and may have discussed it after the coroner's verdict – I expect they didn't want to upset Jamie's mother, especially if their suspicions turned out to be unwarranted.'

'Fair point.'

The wind caught Kay's hair as she climbed from the passenger seat, and she hooked a wayward strand behind her ear before closing the car door.

The sweet stink of manure wafted from a pile that had been stacked next to the barn, and Kay was reminded of horse-riding lessons on holiday as a child. A blue plastic tarpaulin flapped in the breeze, exposing the potent mix of straw and dung.

A machinery shed stretched along the right-hand side of the open space, its wide double doors exposing a gap through which she could see a large green coloured tractor and assorted equipment. The roof looked as if it had been recently repaired in places, with the new corrugated iron a pale contrast to the original.

Somewhere in the distance, she could hear another tractor out in the orchards; a reminder that work on a farm was constant, no matter the season.

She suppressed a smile as Barnes wove his way between waterlogged potholes in the farmyard surface, then turned her attention to the square-shaped Georgian style farmhouse.

She imagined that in the spring it would be an idyllic place, bursting to life as the farm workers strove to make the most of the warmer weather.

Now though, the surrounding land was unwelcoming, a cold chill gripping the countryside.

She shivered as Barnes joined her on the doorstep.

'Ready?'

'Go for it.'

She reached out and pressed the doorbell set into the right-hand side of the frame, straining her ears to hear its dulcet tones sounding within the inner sanctum of the house.

After what seemed an age, she heard footsteps approaching before the door was wrenched open and a man peered out.

His face softened when he saw her, and he extended his hand.

'You must be Detective Inspector Kay Hunter.'

Surprised, she shook his hand before she realised her jaw had dropped. 'Sharp…?'

'Phoned me last night,' he said, and shrugged. 'Probably not protocol, but—'

'You've known each other a long time.'

'Exactly.'

Kay gestured to Barnes and introduced him.

'Come on in – and please, call me Michael.' The farmer stood to one side to let them pass. 'Don't worry about your shoes. We have two Springer spaniels, so you've got nothing to worry about. Let's go through to the kitchen – Bridget has the kettle on.'

Kay followed, Barnes at her heels as Michael Ingram led them along a flagstone hallway.

He wore a battered pair of denim jeans with a worn green jumper, the neck of which exposed a creased shirt collar, and he walked with the gait of a man who didn't like to hang about.

She picked up her pace to keep up with him.

A woman rose from a chair at a six-seater pine dining table as they entered an enormous kitchen that took up the length of two-thirds of the farmhouse.

'This is my wife, Bridget.'

'Thanks for seeing us this morning,' said Kay, shaking hands with the woman.

'Not at all,' said Bridget. 'Please, sit down. You'll have tea?'

'Wonderful,' said Barnes, positioning himself closest to the large Aga stove that abutted the kitchen cabinets.

The two dogs raised their heads from their beds as he sat down, but quickly lost interest once they realised they weren't getting any treats.

Kay waited while the Ingrams fussed around making the drinks, and once they were all settled around the table, she turned her attention to the couple in front of her.

'I'm not sure how much DI Sharp was able to tell you, but I can confirm that on the basis of new information, and in light of other factors, I have been tasked with reopening the investigation into your son Jamie's death.'

Bridget raised a shaking hand to her mouth.

Her husband reached over and wound his fingers

around her other hand before turning his focus to Kay.

'Sharp said that we could count on you.'

'You can.' She swallowed as Michael squeezed his wife's hand, and fought to bury her own memories that threatened to surface. She caught Barnes staring at her, but shook her head.

Now wasn't the time.

'All right then, what new information have you received?'

ELEVEN

'I can't give specific details, because it involves an ongoing internal investigation into other matters. What I can tell you is that my review of the events at the time and this current case review have the full support of my detective chief inspector.'

'So, we could go through all this, and you still might not be able to overturn the coroner's verdict?'

'I'm sorry, yes. That's right. However, I promise you that I'll work diligently with my team, reinterview everyone who knew Jamie at the time, and investigate every angle.'

'Good,' said Bridget. 'I remember the man we spoke to from the police ten years ago. He seemed to have already made his mind up it was an accident, despite what Michael told him at the time.'

She raised her coffee mug to her lips, and appraised Kay over the rim.

Kay relaxed, realising that Jamie's mother had accepted her. She leaned back in her chair, cradling her own mug of tea in her lap. After making sure Barnes was ready to take notes, she began.

'It would be a great help if I could have some background about you, such as where you met and how you adjusted from army life to being on a farm.'

Michael reached out for his wife's hand, and smiled. 'Well, you probably already picked up on Bridget's accent even though she's lived here for the past thirty-five years. I was posted in Germany when I met her. That was back in the eighties. I was based at Rheindahlen for six months, and when my unit returned to England, Bridget came with me. We were married a year later.'

'My parents were mortified,' said Bridget, and managed a small laugh. 'Luckily, we've proved them wrong, and before they died they liked to spend summers here on the farm with us and the children.'

'I understand that you inherited the farm, Michael. How long was that after you had returned from Germany?'

'About nine months. I'd received word from my sister that my father had fallen ill, and we knew in our hearts that he didn't have long. I spoke to my commanding officer, and we agreed that I would resign my commission in order to take over the running of the farm. My sister had no interest in the business – she lives in Scotland and had two small children at the time.' He shrugged. 'It was natural for me to take over the family business.'

'When did Jamie come along?'

'We'd lived here for a year or so when I found out I was expecting,' said Bridget. 'Finding out I was carrying twins was a bit of a shock – the harvest hadn't been good that year, and money was tight.'

Michael picked up the story. 'I managed to borrow a bit of money from the bank to see us through. Luckily, I was able to pay off that loan in full the next year, but looking back it was quite a scary time for us.'

'I'd imagine it must have been quite a juggling act for you, managing a farm with two small children running around,' said Kay.

'Except you don't think about it at the time,' said Bridget. 'Looking back now, it seems quite idyllic, but you're right – it was bloody hard work.'

Kay placed her mug on the table and reached for her notebook, flipping through the pages.

'I don't recall the fact that Jamie and his sister

being twins was captured in the original statements.'

'That shows you how much notice the investigating detective gave to the case,' said Bridget. 'We did tell him, although Natalie has slightly darker hair than her brother, and she is quite different in personality.'

'Headstrong,' said Michael. He wore a rueful smile. 'And she still manages to wind me around her little finger.'

'How did she and Jamie get on?'

'They were very close. When Jamie got into his motorcycling, Natalie was often the one building makeshift jumps and helping him build bridges over streams around here so he could test his skills.'

'I'll need to speak with Natalie, along with Jamie's friends, but could you take me through the days leading up to his death?'

Michael sighed, and pushed his coffee mug away. 'I suppose it's all hindsight, but something seemed to be troubling him. He'd returned from Afghanistan a couple of weeks before, and we didn't see him for a few days. When he did turn up here, he seemed distracted and unable to settle.'

'We tried talking to him,' said Bridget, 'but he wouldn't tell us what was going on. At first, I thought he might be embarrassed about something that had happened – maybe he'd split up with a girl or something. I got more concerned as the days passed, because he seemed to retreat within himself. He'd mope around the farm, refusing to help Michael. I'd find him standing there, at the kitchen sink, staring into space through the window. I asked him what was the matter, but he wouldn't tell me.'

She broke off, and sniffed.

'Was he ever treated for post-traumatic stress disorder?'

'No – luckily for us, he never went out on patrol,' said Michael. 'His role was in supply and logistics, so he was always at the base. His job was to ensure the vehicles and equipment were available at all times, and kept in good condition.'

'Did he talk to his sister at all during this time?'

'Yes,' said Michael. 'Natalie was here three days before Jamie died. She tried her best to pull him out of his mood as well, but it seemed like she only made it worse. They had an argument late that afternoon – I didn't hear what it was about, but knowing Natalie she was probably nagging him.' He shrugged. 'She's not the most patient of people, and I think perhaps she might have had a go at him. Anyway, it ended with her storming out the door, and Jamie didn't bother going after her.'

'Did they argue often?'

'They'd bicker, like any siblings do,' said Bridget. 'That was more like what happened. It didn't seem like a huge argument. Just raised voices. I know Natalie was devastated when Jamie died – their last words were spoken in anger, after all.'

'I'm sorry, I know this is difficult for you. On the day Jamie died, did anything unusual happen?'

Michael sighed. 'We told the detective at the time. Jamie got a call on his mobile phone late that night while he was still here. He wouldn't say who it was from afterwards, and when he saw the number on the screen he went outside to answer it. I've got no idea what was said, but when he came back inside he looked physically sick. His face was pale, and I noticed his hands were shaking.'

Bridget dabbed a tissue at her eyes. 'He wouldn't talk to us for the rest of the night. He disappeared up to his room, and I could hear him moving around. I went upstairs an hour later, and when I tapped on his door he told me to go away.' She sniffed. 'The last time we saw him, we were watching the television – I was watching the end of an old black and white film. He stuck his head around the door to the living room and said he was going out for a while, and that he didn't know when he would be back.'

'The police turned up here at five o'clock in the morning. We'd just had a cup of tea when they knocked on the door and we found out that Jamie had been killed. He hadn't been carrying any identification on him, and there'd been a delay checking the registration details for the motorbike while he'd been rushed to hospital. By the time they tracked down our names and address, it was too late – he'd already passed away from the extent of his injuries.'

Michael reached across and pulled a paper tissue from a box, and blew his nose.

Kay gave them a moment to compose themselves, and then consulted her notes.

'Can I ask – after the inquest, was Jamie's mobile phone returned to you?'

'Yes,' said Bridget. 'I was loath to throw anything away of his, but in the end, we decided we had to move on – he was never coming back, was he?'

Kay's heart sank. 'And the phone?'

'We donated it to one of those recycling charities about three years after he died,' said Michael. 'I think we realised we were struggling to carry on with our lives without him, and so we spent a weekend together sorting out his old bedroom here.'

Bridget managed a small smile. 'It brought the

two of us closer together. I wouldn't wish anyone to go through what we did, but we had to let him go.'

Kay rechecked her notes and, satisfied she'd covered everything, raised her gaze to the Ingrams. 'Michael, Bridget, thank you very much for taking the time to speak with us today. I appreciate it's difficult to talk about Jamie after all this time.'

'Detective, please be careful when speaking with our daughter. She took Jamie's death very hard,' said Michael.

'They were very close, you see,' said Bridget. 'Natalie lost all contact with her friends. She retreated into herself for a long time afterwards. She had to have three months of counselling to help with her grief after the accident.'

'I understand. I'll bear that in mind.' Kay pushed back her chair, and signalled to Barnes the interview was over.

Michael led them back to the front door, and stood on the threshold for a moment before turning to Kay.

'Find out who killed my son, Detective. Someone out there knows something, and his killer has been walking around free for ten years.'

'I'll do everything I can, Mr Ingram.'

TWELVE

Barnes slowed the car as he entered Yalding village, then braked as they approached a narrow bridge that crossed the River Beult before it joined the larger River Medway.

He drummed his fingers on the steering wheel while he waited for traffic to travel from the opposite direction, cursing under his breath as a bus passed too close for comfort.

'At least the river didn't flood this winter,' said Kay. 'For a moment over Christmas, I thought all of this would be under water again.'

As the last vehicle passed his window, Barnes slipped the car into gear and accelerated. 'I haven't been here in years. Where does Natalie Ingram live?'

'Her married name is Stockton. She and her husband have a house on Vicarage Lane.'

She peered across him at the large fifteenth-century church that dominated the boundary of the village, its ragstone and sandstone brickwork contrasting with the dark skies above.

'Down here, on the right.'

As they progressed along the lane, the houses to each side grew larger and became spaced further apart from their neighbours.

'They must be doing all right for themselves if they can afford to live down this end of the village,' said Barnes.

'At the time of Jamie's death, Natalie was working in financial regulation in the City. I'm not sure what she's doing now, but I expect she was earning some serious money back then.'

She paused, and gestured out of the window. 'It's this one, coming up on the left.'

Two brick pillars supported a black wrought iron gate, which was open and led through to a circular gravel driveway. In the middle of the circle stood an ornamental fountain and pampas grass. The ostentatiousness of the setting was softened by a selection of children's outdoor toys that lay strewn across the central grass area.

Kay turned her attention to the house – with gables overhanging the front windows and a porch that jutted out from the front door, she reckoned it had been built in the 1930s, and then improved upon over the years.

'Nice place,' said Barnes.

Kay's mouth twitched as he stopped the engine and opened his door.

'Nice driveway, too. You won't get your shoes muddy this time.'

He stuck two fingers up at her before slamming the door, and she laughed.

A harried-looking woman peered out of the window to the right-hand side of the porch, and Kay heard footsteps before Barnes had a chance to reach out for the doorbell.

When the door opened, the woman stood on the threshold, her hair arranged in a messy topknot that threatened to escape.

She wore a blue denim shirt over black leggings, with colourful socks covering her feet, and extended her hand before Kay managed to open her mouth.

'Natalie Stockton. Mum and Dad said that you'd be on your way over.'

Kay recognised anticipation in the woman's voice,

and introduced herself and Barnes. 'May we come in?'

'Of course. Let's go through to the office. It's a bit of a mess, I'm afraid. I've got two massive commissions that are both due this week.'

Kay's eyes travelled over the tasteful decor as she followed Natalie into the room at the front of the house to her right.

They entered what Natalie had called the office – essentially a living room that had been taken over and put to a different use.

The walls had been painted a shade of off-white, complemented by artwork and bric-à-brac that she suspected didn't come from the local department store. The effect could have been pretentious, but was saved by the children's paintings that had been framed and hung next to the professional offerings. A bespoke desk took up the length of one wall, its surface hidden beneath scraps of material, sketchbooks, and interior decor magazines.

Natalie waved them to a two-seater sofa under the window. 'Make yourself comfortable. Did you want anything to drink?'

'No, that's fine, thanks. And thank you for seeing us without an appointment. We appreciate it.'

Natalie reached out for the chair next to the desk

and spun it around until she faced the two detectives. She sat down with a sigh, and pushed a wayward strand of hair off her forehead.

'That's okay – I could do with a break from the computer and everything. Sometimes I find hours have gone by and I've been hunched up over my work. Then I wonder why I have a bad back.' She smiled. 'After I had the kids, I got bored, so I started my own interior design business. It's like they always say, you're only stressed when you're busy, not so much when there's no work about.'

Barnes rummaged in his pocket for his notebook and opened it. 'Do you mind if I ask what sort of clients you work for?'

'Not at all. It's mostly home styling for magazines. Sometimes I'm asked to style whole houses – rental properties for example, when owners want to ensure they get the best sale price possible by making rooms look perfect, with beautifully made beds, lovely materials, immaculate decor. Basically, nothing like what this place looks like when the kids are around.'

'I'd imagine you've got your hands full running a business from home with two young children.'

'Oh God, yeah. Luckily, they go to nursery three days a week now.'

'I understand from the original statement you gave that you worked in financial regulation in the City. Do you miss it?'

'Hell, no.' She choked out a laugh. 'Way too stressful, and very chauvinistic. Quitting that job was the best thing I ever did. I don't even keep in touch with the people I used to work with. I'm much happier doing something creative.'

'What does your husband do?'

'Giles? He still works in the City – he's an economist with one of the American banks. Thankfully, he's been quite high up in that role for a few years now, so he only has to commute during the week. It means he can spend time with the kids at the weekends.'

'How long have you been married?'

Natalie smiled. 'Six years. We've known each other for eight, but it took him a while to pluck up the courage to ask me, I think.'

Kay grew serious. 'As I said to your mum and dad, I'm sorry that we have to disturb you this morning, and that some of our questions may upset you, but we've been authorised to take another look at Jamie's motorcycle accident.'

'Can I ask why?'

'I can't divulge operational issues, but I can say

that this investigation stems from an ongoing internal audit process.'

'Okay.'

'We may have more questions in later days as we learn more about Jamie and the circumstances of his accident, but for the time being could you tell me what you argued about with him, the last time you saw him?'

Natalie's shoulders slumped. 'It was stupid, really. Especially after what happened. I was trying to organise a surprise party for our parents' wedding anniversary, and attempting to coordinate it so that Jamie could be there. He was only back for a few weeks, and I knew if he returned to Afghanistan, it could be another six months before we saw him again. I wanted to have the party before he went back.' She emitted a shaking breath, tears threatening. 'He was being a pain, to be honest. He had no interest in helping me, and said it was better if I sorted it out. He offered to go halves with the finances, of course, but he wasn't being the most sociable of people. He seemed distracted, almost as if he had more important things to do.'

'Why did you feel you couldn't talk to your parents about it after he died?'

'I blamed myself partly for his accident – he went

out of his way to avoid me after we argued, and I didn't want to spoil his time with our parents, so I didn't go to the farmhouse again while he was there.'

'You say that he wasn't the most outgoing of people at that time. Did you know any of his friends?'

'When we were growing up, yes. After he joined the army, he seemed to grow distant. The times he did visit, he'd meet up with one or two of them for a drink, but it didn't seem that he had anything in common with them anymore. I think he had a couple of friends in the army – people he worked with – but that's about it.'

'Did you stay in touch with any of his friends after he died?'

Natalie shook her head. 'Mum and Dad probably told you, but I was in a pretty bad way after Jamie died. I had to seek counselling for a little while to help with the grief. They always say twins are closer than normal siblings, don't they? Maybe that's what made it so hard.'

'I understand this is difficult for you, and again I'm sorry I have to ask these questions, but can you think of anyone that would have wanted to harm Jamie?'

'Harm him? What do you mean?'

'Please, just answer the question.'

'No, I can't imagine anyone wanting to harm him. Dad was the one who's always been convinced there was someone else involved in Jamie's accident, but Jamie wasn't the sort of person who got into trouble. Even at school, he kept his nose clean. It was usually me that got the detentions or the extra homework.'

Kay closed her notebook, and rose from the sofa. 'I think that will do for now, but here's my business card. I'll keep you informed of any developments, but in the meantime if you remember anything that you think might help us, please call.'

'I will, thanks.'

She showed them out to the hallway, and shook hands.

'Detective Hunter, I realise you have a hard job to do given the time that's passed since Jamie died, but please know it's important to me to learn the truth.'

Kay peered over her shoulder to where Barnes was making his way towards the car, then turned back to Natalie, and offered her a reassuring smile.

'It's important to me, too.'

THIRTEEN

By the time the team convened for the day's briefing, darkness had cloaked the county town for over two hours.

Kay suppressed a yawn as Gavin and Carys filed into Sharp's office, and resolved to keep the meeting short.

She waited until Debbie had closed the door before she began her summary of the two interviews she and Barnes had conducted earlier that day.

'So, it seems that his family noticed that he had something else on his mind when he returned from Afghanistan, but he didn't speak to anybody about what was bothering him. Michael and Bridget Ingram confirmed that the night of his death Jamie received a phone call, which he answered in private. He never told them who the caller was, or what that conversation was about. Natalie Ingram confirms that after she and her brother had argued three days before that, they didn't speak again.'

'Did they happen to mention whether he seemed scared?' said Carys.

'Natalie didn't, but her parents certainly noticed the change in Jamie after that call,' said Barnes. 'It seems he refused to tell them what it was about, and they didn't press the matter.'

'Anyway,' said Kay. 'What did the rest of you manage to get done today? Any progress?'

Gavin held up a printout. 'Debbie and I have been going through the list of Jamie's friends and acquaintances from the original investigation, and we've updated that with phone numbers and new addresses where people have moved.'

'I've left a message with the barracks where Jamie was based,' said Carys. 'It took a bit of work, but I finally managed to find out where his commanding officer is working these days, and I've left a message for him to call me as a matter of urgency. As soon as he does, I'll arrange a meeting for us to go and speak with him.'

'Great work,' said Kay.

'I also got in touch with the personnel department

here, and they've given me the contact details for the forensic collision investigator who attended the scene of Jamie's accident. I've forwarded the email to you.'

'Fantastic, thanks. Okay, these are our next steps. Gavin and Carys – can you go through that list of Jamie's friends and acquaintances, note any questions to get us started, and divide them up between us so we can start re-interviewing them as soon as possible? We'll work in pairs for the interviews, so that means we're going to have to conduct them in between everything else that's on our desks out there. Put the ones who previously gave statements at the top, and everyone else after that. Debbie – once that's done, can you start making phone calls to arrange times for us to meet with those people?'

She turned her attention to Barnes, but he put up his hand.

'Sorry, Kay – I've got to be at the magistrates' court tomorrow, and possibly the next day. It's the hearing for a case we closed back in November.'

She raised an eyebrow. 'Seems like the backlog hasn't improved since I was last here.'

'Got that right.'

Kay stifled another yawn. 'All right. We'll skip the briefing tomorrow – you've all got plenty to do.

We'll meet again the day after tomorrow and see what progress we've made then.'

'What about you, Kay?'

She dropped the pen onto the metal shelf under the whiteboard and turned to Barnes.

'I'm going to try to arrange to meet with the original forensic collision investigator from Traffic tomorrow morning to find out what he thought about Jamie's accident.'

———

The next day, Kay stood in a potholed lay-by at the side of the A20, her umbrella doing little to ward off the effects of a late winter downpour that was driving horizontal rain at her face.

She extended her hand to the man who jogged towards her after parking his car, the hood of his jacket obscuring his face until he drew close.

'Jeff Bishop,' he said, before shoving his hands back into his jacket pockets.

'Thanks for meeting me. I half expected you to cancel.'

He shrugged. 'I used to be out in all weathers. To be honest, I'd rather be here – the wife has me retiling the bathroom at the moment.'

Kay smiled. 'I appreciate it.'

'No problem. Where do you want to start?'

'I've read through your original report a few times, but it would be useful if you could walk me through the scene of the accident when you first attended. As I said on the phone last night, I've been tasked with reviewing the case in light of new information, and it's a lot easier for me to do so if I can visualise what everything looked like that night rather than trying to work it out from a report.'

'Have you been talking to Sharp?'

Kay took a step back in surprise, and he rolled his eyes.

'You have, haven't you? You know he's been running with the theory of foul play ever since that accident? It got to the point where I used to try and avoid him at the Christmas parties.'

She opened her mouth to protest, and then noticed the corner of his eyes crinkle with amusement.

'It's all right,' he said, and jerked his thumb over his shoulder. 'Come on. We need to start over there, down by the junction to Ulcombe.'

Kay locked her car and trudged after him. She scowled as a dark blue panel van shot past them, sending the contents of a large puddle over her shoes and the hem of her trousers.

Bishop set a fast pace, retreating to the grass verge whenever a vehicle approached, and then taking off once more when it was safe to do so.

The Ulcombe turn-off was less than a quarter of mile away, and they paused at the road sign next to the T-junction.

'This is where he would have started his approach into the bend,' said Bishop. 'As you can see, the main road begins to rise from here, so he would have started to accelerate. The weather that night was similar to this, so visibility would have been reduced. Have you ever been on a motorbike?'

'No.'

'Okay, well I can tell you – when it's pissing down with rain like it is today, it's not a lot of fun. They've made improvements to visors on helmets, but it's not just the rainwater dashing against that, you've got to imagine the noise of a heavy downpour on your head. I don't care what people say, it doesn't matter how good a motorcyclist you are – conditions like this impede your ability to react, because your senses are being battered.'

'Was there any indication that he was speeding?'

'It's likely, given the number of infringements recorded on his licence. As you'll know from the file, there were no witnesses, so that's conjecture on my part.'

'So, he's lined himself up to take the corner. What happens next?'

Bishop looked to his right and then left, before beckoning Kay across the road. 'Come on, we'll walk the route.'

Kay was grateful that a proper path had been constructed on the opposite side of the road, making it easier to keep up with Bishop. She paused to scrape the worst of the mud off her boots, and then caught up with him as he stopped at the crest of the hill.

'This is where it all went wrong. You've heard about the point of no return with regard to aircraft?'

'No, I haven't.'

'It's when an aircraft is taking off. The pilot has got a split second before the front wheels leave the ground to abort the take-off. Once the nose of the plane lifts into the air, there's no turning back. It's like that when you steer a motorbike around a bend. After you've committed to the manoeuvre, you can't simply steer the other way if something goes wrong. Any deviation to your riding line, and the machine is going to flip out from underneath you. Watch some motorbike racing on the television sometime – you'll see what I mean.'

He pointed to the road surface.

'And, before you ask, we assessed the road conditions that night. There was no oil on the asphalt at the point at which he lost control, and there were no potholes that could have thrown him off course. The only oil traces were from where his bike hit the ground and slid across to the other side.'

'So, given that Jamie had a reputation for being such a good motorcyclist, even if he did like to speed, what do you think went wrong?'

He shrugged. 'It's like I said in my report. He knew this road really well – perhaps too well. He was accelerating, the weather was atrocious, and he simply misjudged the corner.'

'What if he had to swerve at the last minute to avoid hitting something?'

'No. It's like I stated in my report. If a rabbit ran out in front of him, we would have found the body. If he collided with a deer, there would have been significant damage to the motorbike over and above that caused by the impact of it hitting the road. And again, if that happened then it's likely we would have found the body of the deer close by. We didn't find anything.'

Kay shook her head. 'That's not what I meant.

What if a car pulled out in front of him and he tried to swerve to avoid it?'

Bishop scratched his chin and cast his eyes along the stretch of road. 'There were no skid marks or debris from any other vehicles in the vicinity. We checked.'

'What if the driver had no intention of braking?'

His head snapped around, his eyes meeting hers. 'A hit-and-run, you mean?'

'Maybe, or perhaps he was targeted deliberately.'

Bishop raised his eyes to the grey sky, and then he pointed at their cars further up the road.

'There's a decent pub on the lane up to Ulcombe. Let's go there and get out of this weather. You can buy me a pint and explain yourself.'

FOURTEEN

Bishop took a swig from his pint, then set the glass down on the table between them, smacking his lips.

When Kay had followed his vehicle into the car park outside, she had peered through the windscreen at the sweeping view across a sodden field, and tried to imagine what the place would look like in summer.

As the rainfall intensified, she gave up, launched herself from the car and hurried after Bishop.

Inside, the pub provided a respite from the elements, and they had timed their visit to perfection – the premises had opened only half an hour before, ready to welcome anyone brave enough to venture out for lunch.

Horse brasses adorned the inglenook fireplace, while the walls of the pub held framed photographs of the local area through the ages. Dried hops hugged the supporting beams, and the faint sound of a radio station filtered through from the kitchen.

Bishop had waved her over to the two sofas next to the fireplace, and ordered their drinks before sinking onto the sofa opposite her. He ran a hand through his grey hair, which was wet despite the waterproofs he'd worn.

Kay sipped at her lemonade and cast her eyes around the pub while she savoured the warmth from the open fire. She realised she probably looked like a drowned rat herself, and slid her feet across the carpet to try and dry out her boots.

She turned at the sound of a short, sharp bark, then leaned over and held out her hand to a Jack Russell terrier who hurried over from behind the bar. She ruffled its ears before turning her attention back to Bishop.

'I'd forgotten about this place – I don't think I've been here in years.'

'They do a great Sunday lunch. It's still owned by the same family that bought the place back in the 1950s, too. Perfect on a day like this.'

He adjusted his waterproof coat on the arm of the sofa and then, once satisfied it wasn't going to slide onto the floor, picked up his glass.

'All right. Explain to me where the hell you got the idea that Jamie was the victim of a hit and run.'

She sighed, then leaned forward and rested her elbows on her knees. She glanced over to the bar, but there was no-one within earshot.

'It's been going around in my mind for about a day, ever since I spoke with his parents and sister and read through the original file. I mean, both his parents and Sharp have been telling me what a great motorcyclist he was and how well he knew the roads around here. So, how come he got killed?'

'Bad luck.'

'Oh, come on! Surely you don't believe that?'

He put his glass on the table, half full. 'I do, actually. You can be the best driver – or rider – in the world, and still come unstuck. Trust me, I've seen so many cases where vehicles have ended up in impossible positions, and you stand there, staring at it, trying to work out how the hell it happened. I've managed investigations where drivers have lost control and ended upside down in trees at the side of the road, for goodness' sakes. Luck plays a huge role in our lives every day.'

Kay chewed her lip. 'Was there any indication that Jamie's motorbike had been tampered with?'

'None whatsoever. We tore that thing apart in the

workshop. We had to – we had Sharp's army police nagging us, as well as Harrison's team. At the end of the day though, it was rider error.'

She turned her glass in the condensation it had created on the surface of the table, before lifting her gaze as Bishop slid across a cardboard coaster with a brewery logo emblazoned across it.

'I used to work behind a bar at university. You wouldn't believe what a pain that is, clearing up the mess people make.'

He winked, and she grinned in return.

'How did you become a forensic crash investigator?'

'I fell into it, really. I studied engineering at university – that's when I was working in bars to earn a bit of money on the side – and I enjoyed the physics side of the engineering degree as well. I don't like the cold, so when I graduated I didn't fancy doing what most of my contemporaries were doing – heading up to Aberdeen to work on some of the big gas projects – and I saw an advertisement for a junior investigator at a private consulting firm in Hertfordshire. I always liked messing about with my own cars, and my father was a mechanic, so it was a logical step, I suppose. What about you? Why did you join the police?'

She shrugged. 'I like problem solving, and I like the challenges the role brings.'

'I saw the story in the newspaper about you before Christmas,' he said. 'You nearly died.'

She shivered. 'Nearly. Not an experience I want to repeat any time soon, I can assure you.'

'Well, I have to admit that if it was anyone else who asked me to do this in my free time, the answer would've been no.' He gestured towards her with his glass. 'You, however, have a reputation for tenacity, and that's a tough quality to hold on to in this day and age.'

She watched as he took a sip. 'Thank you.'

He suppressed a belch, and placed the empty glass at the end of the table. 'You're welcome.'

'Going back to Jamie. You're convinced another vehicle didn't strike him, but what if someone deliberately made him swerve?'

'How?'

'If someone was approaching from the opposite direction – from the Leeds roundabout – and swerved into the path of Jamie's motorbike, he'd have nowhere to go.'

'How would they know it was him? It was dark, remember?'

'What if they were expecting him?'

'Even if they did, he'd have seen the car approaching – the headlights would've reflected off the trees as they drew closer.'

'What if they didn't have their headlights switched on?'

Bishop gave a low whistle through his teeth. 'You are one devious thinker, Hunter.'

Kay drained her lemonade before setting her glass on the table. 'Is it possible that's what could've happened?'

'Maybe. Yes, it's possible.'

'So, now we have a scenario where Jamie Ingram may have been killed intentionally, based on the fact you're saying it's possible he may have swerved to avoid an oncoming vehicle. The driver of which didn't stop at the time, or come forward during the investigation.'

'Hey, I only said maybe.'

'I know.' She glanced over her shoulder and turned her attention to the road beyond the front door of the pub at the sound of an engine as a motorbike tore past, and then turned back to Bishop.

'Makes you wonder though, doesn't it?'

FIFTEEN

The following Monday, Kay eased herself from the passenger seat of the car, and began to weave her way between the other vehicles parked in front of the administrative block of Worthy Down Barracks, Carys at her heels.

She rolled her neck, easing out the kinks that had formed during the early morning journey from Kent to the depths of Hampshire.

Carys had elected to drive, collecting Kay from her house while it was still dark.

'You drive on the way back,' she'd said. 'I can use the time to type up my notes on my laptop.'

She had phoned Kay the night before, having tracked down Jamie Ingram's old commanding officer over the weekend.

After a promotion and two further deployments, the man had undertaken a teaching position at the Defence College of Logistics, Policing and Administration, and Carys had arranged to interview him between classes.

Kay pushed through the glass door to the building, holding it open for Carys before they made their way to a reception desk.

A young man in fatigues finished a phone call as they approached.

'Can I help you?'

'DI Hunter and DC Miles. We're here to see Colonel Stephen Carterton. He's expecting us.'

'Have a seat over there. I'll let him know you're here.'

As Carys reached into her bag and set her mobile phone to silent mode before pulling out her notebook and a pen, Kay gazed around the room.

An original painting of a desert scene hung on the wall behind the reception desk, depicting a tank in desert colours bursting over a dune at speed, the artist capturing the dust and heat perfectly. To the right of her, a large wooden frame held a brass plaque that listed all the commanding officers of the various regiments now based at the barracks.

The decor appeared to have been polished to

within an inch of its life, and she reckoned the soldier behind the desk would have a fit if he saw the state of the incident room back at Maidstone.

If she worked here, she'd be afraid to touch anything for fear of smearing or breaking it.

Five minutes later, and precisely at the time that had been set for their meeting, a tall man in matching fatigues to those of the soldier at the desk appeared at the end of the corridor next to the reception area.

His fair-coloured hair was cropped in a style similar to Sharp's normal cut, and his skin bore the traces of a long time spent in harsh sunlight in far-flung places. He strode across the tiled floor with an air of efficiency, a man comfortable with the rank he now held.

'You're from Kent Police?'

Kay held out her hand. 'DI Hunter. You spoke with my colleague, DC Miles, yesterday.'

Stephen Carterton shook hands with both of them, and gestured to them to follow him.

'You're lucky. This week is the calm before the storm.'

Kay's eyes narrowed as he held open the door to their left, and motioned them to two seats opposite a desk.

'What do you mean?'

He smiled. 'Exam week starts next week. Stressful enough for the students, even more stressful for us tutors.' He pushed aside a pile of paperwork and a computer keyboard and then rested his arms on the desk. 'Now, how can I help you?'

'As DC Miles told you, I've reopened an investigation into the death of Jamie Ingram. New evidence has come to light, and we're revisiting the witness statements from that time.'

Carterton ran a hand over his jaw. 'That was a nasty business. Motorbike accident, wasn't it?'

'That's right. We're trying to learn more about Jamie and his role in the Royal Logistics Corps, as well as speaking to family and friends. Can I ask what your role was at the time? I realise you provided a witness statement, but it's useful to go over the information.'

'Of course. I was a lieutenant colonel at the time, and commanding officer for the regiment – we were responsible for the management of critical spares to the brigade and the deployed forces around the world. As you can imagine, when we're based in places such as Afghanistan, the wear and tear on equipment and vehicles can be catastrophic.'

'When did you first meet Jamie?'

'He came straight to us from basic training. I

think his background – the farm, I mean – gave him a natural ability for planning and logistical work. It was almost second nature to him.'

'What was his role?'

'He was one of a number of people who managed the return of damaged parts, sourced replacements, and carried out all the administrative responsibilities associated with that. We use systems similar to logistics companies all over the world – it's all computerised, and we provided an end to end service.'

'So, there would be a paper trail for every piece of equipment?'

'That's right, yes.'

'Were any anomalies discovered in the system during Jamie's time?'

Carterton leaned back in his chair and assessed her. 'Now, what would make you say that?'

Her heart skipped a beat, before she forced a smile. 'I believe I'm the one asking the questions today. Were there any anomalies?'

'Nothing that we could prove. It was unlike him, too. When he joined us, he was extremely diligent in his work and respected by those who worked with him.'

'What changed?'

'I'm not sure. It seemed to tie in with his third or fourth deployment to Afghanistan. Obviously, it's a stressful situation for any soldier, but Jamie was never exposed to any fighting. His role was back at base, helping to ensure that those on the frontline were properly equipped, and if something was broken, it got replaced or repaired as soon as possible. When he came back from that deployment, he seemed different.'

'In what way?'

'Cocky, rather than self-assured. As if he knew something no-one else did. His changing attitude alienated him from a lot of his peers. It got worse as time went on.'

'How many times was he deployed before he died?'

'About four or five in total.'

Kay flipped through her notes. 'We'll be talking to his friends and colleagues over the course of the next few days. Did he have any close friends within the Corps?'

'Well, despite putting a few noses out of joint with his attitude, he remained close to two men that he served with. Carl Ashton and Glenn Boyd.'

'You say that he appeared cocky. Did you notice anything else?'

'Come to think of it, yes. In the weeks before he died, his work began to get sloppy, which was unusual for him. It was almost as if he had something on his mind all the time. He seemed to find it hard to concentrate. Like I said, he wasn't like that when he first joined us.'

Kay closed her notebook. 'It seems strange that in the space of a year or so, Jamie Ingram changed from being the perfect soldier to one that couldn't care less about his work.'

Carterton gave a mirthless laugh. 'He wasn't a perfect soldier, Detective. Didn't Sharp tell you that Jamie Ingram was under investigation for dealing Class A drugs?'

SIXTEEN

Kay stood on the doorstep to Sharp's house, fuming.

She and Carys had arrived back in Maidstone two hours before, and after returning the keys for the pool car to Sergeant Hughes on the front desk, she had sent Carys home and then made her way up to the incident room.

She had paced in front of the whiteboard in Sharp's office, her fists clenched as she processed the revelation Jamie's ex-commanding officer had provided.

Finally, she had snatched her bag from the desk and stormed from the building, phoning Adam to let him know she would be home late.

A shadow appeared behind the frosted glass to the

front door a split second before a light flickered to life above her head, and the door opened.

Sharp's jaw clenched when he saw her. 'Hunter. I didn't expect to see you tonight.'

She glared at him. 'You've got some explaining to do.'

She saw his shoulders rise as he took a deep breath.

'Rebecca's out to dinner with some work colleagues. Come on through.'

She stomped over the threshold, then waited while he shut the front door and followed him through to the kitchen.

'Do you want a glass of wine?'

'No, I do not want a bloody glass of wine.'

He turned and folded his arms across his chest. 'Okay. What's going on?'

'I've spent the afternoon talking with Jamie's ex-commanding officer, Stephen Carterton. Why didn't you tell me you were investigating Jamie for supplying Class A drugs?'

'Because I wanted you to carry out your own investigation. To see if you came up with another reason for his death.'

She took a deep breath. 'Tell me everything you know about Jamie Ingram. All of it, this time.'

He waved her over to a circular table that took up one corner of the kitchen and waited until she sat before he pulled out a chair opposite hers and sank into it.

'I didn't want to believe it at the time,' he said, staring at the tiled floor. 'I'd known him since he was a toddler. Watched him grow into a young man. He was smart, hardworking, and kind. You don't see those qualities in enough people these days. I never told you, but Rebecca and I could never have kids, so Jamie and Natalie became favourites of ours.'

Kay emitted a groan. 'So, when I was going through everything last year, that must've hit a nerve. Why didn't you tell me, Devon?'

'You said it yourself. You had enough to worry about. Surely you must've wondered, though.'

'I always presumed the photos on the shelf in the living room were ones of your kids.'

'Michael and Bridget asked us to be godparents to Jamie and Natalie when they were born. We couldn't say no.'

Kay inched forward on her chair. 'All right. Back to Jamie and the drugs. When did you first suspect something?'

'About a week after he returned from Afghanistan – it was his fourth tour there – he turned up on our doorstep with a new motorbike. I asked him about the finance on it, and he laughed and said he'd bought it outright. It worried me for days afterwards – I knew he'd never be able to afford that on an army wage. I made some discreet enquiries when I got back onto barracks the next day, and it turned out the bike wasn't the only thing Jamie had purchased that week – one of the girls who worked at the pub near the married quarters was showing off an expensive-looking pair of diamond earrings. Apparently, Jamie had bought them for her. I didn't even know he was going out with her.'

'So, he was flashing his money around to impress everyone, you mean?'

'Exactly.'

'Carterton told us that Jamie's attitude changed, too – he was starting to verge on the point of being arrogant.'

'That's true. And again, out of character for him. It was almost as if he thought the army wasn't good enough for him anymore.'

'What did you do?'

'I began to watch him more closely. Back then, the Royal Logistics Corps was based at Deepcut in Surrey. Jamie used to travel from there to his parents' farm in Kent when he was on leave – I think he liked the familiarity of the place in between postings, and I know Michael was always grateful for the extra pair of hands. This time, Jamie didn't go to the farm. He hung around the barracks, as if he was waiting for something.'

'Or someone.'

'Yes. Anyway, about three days before he was due to ship back to Afghanistan, he got a phone call from his sister. It was Bridget's birthday, and Natalie had arranged a surprise party for her. Rebecca and I were invited as well, so I was able to keep an eye on Jamie without him suspecting me.' He sighed, and straightened. 'Anyway, nothing happened then. It all kicked off when he came back six months later.'

'What happened?'

'A container load of parts was returned from the frontline to be reconditioned. I was in my office on barracks that morning, and suddenly all hell broke loose – there were dogs barking, people shouting. I ran outside to see what was going on, to find that the container had been unsealed in the logistics area, and two of the drug dogs were going crazy. Jamie was there, along with another private, and their faces were absolutely ashen.'

'Drugs?'

'Hidden in the empty fuel tank from a Jackal – a

four-by-four vehicle the Royal Logistics Corps uses in Afghanistan.'

'How much?'

'Enough.'

Kay's lips thinned. 'Official Secrets Act?'

'No. Need to know.'

'You're joking, right? Devon, I'm trying to help you out here. How much?'

'Just under half a kilo of cocaine.'

Kay felt her jaw drop. 'Jesus. What happened next?'

'We locked the place down, conducted a search of all the dormitories – turned them upside down, in fact. And the married quarters, including mine. Jamie and the other private, a guy by the name of Carl Ashton, were interviewed – extensively, I might add – but we had nothing on them. We found no money, no evidence of who might be involved, nothing. Jamie denied everything, and of course because he was only responsible for opening the container in the first place under observation, we couldn't lay charges without evidence.'

He folded his hands on the table. 'Jamie died two weeks later.'

'Who else did you suspect at the time?'

'The private that was opening the container with

Jamie – Carl. He must've had some help higher up, too, to get everything through the checks the first time. I never suspected Carterton, but I had my doubts about his adjutant, Glenn Boyd.'

'Why didn't you pursue this after Jamie died?'

'We never discovered how they were doing it. We couldn't prove anything. After that incident, no drugs were ever discovered again. Jamie had to have been the ringleader.'

'But Harrison is right, then – you did cover up the information about your investigation when Jamie died?'

'Wrong, Hunter. I didn't cover anything up. At the risk of losing a long-time friend in Michael, I told Harrison about our concerns, but he wasn't interested because we had no proof and he couldn't be bothered to look into it himself. That's why Jamie's death was ruled as accidental – no-one ever pursued the fact that his death could have been caused by someone else.'

'You didn't raise it when you joined Kent Police.'

He slammed his palm on the worktop, his eyes blazing.

'Because Harrison was still a senior officer and would override me. The only reason I told you about this whole mess in the first place was because you demanded to know why Harrison has a vendetta against me. If he's going to try and drag my name through the mud in order to get us back for his being investigated for his conduct over the Jozef Demiri case, then I want to make sure his abominable handling of Jamie's death is sorted out once and for all. I want my job back.'

Kay leaned back on the chair, stunned.

'Bloody hell, Devon.'

SEVENTEEN

Kay paced the room, unable to sit still at her desk.

She checked her watch. Barnes and Gavin had been summoned to a safety demonstration, and wouldn't be back for another half an hour.

Their frustration had been palpable.

She had arrived at the station early that morning, wanting to speak to the small team in private about the direction the investigation had taken, but so far other work commitments had prevented any of them having the time.

She sighed, and made her way to Sharp's office. Standing in front of the whiteboard, she wrote the names Stephen Carterton had given her the previous day on the right-hand side of the board, and began to strategize how to proceed.

She turned at the sound of voices as Barnes pushed through the door and held it open for Carys and Gavin.

'Big fat waste of time that was,' he said. 'What's the point in a safety demonstration of new stab vests when we still have to use the old ones for another six months?'

'Glad I missed the invite,' said Kay. 'Take a seat. There have been some interesting developments.'

She waited while they settled before taking a deep breath.

'It transpires that Jamie Ingram was under investigation for drug dealing.'

Barnes and Gavin swore under their breath.

'Where did you get that from?' said Gavin.

'Jamie's old commanding officer told us, and Sharp confirmed it. Turns out, they didn't have enough evidence to charge Jamie at the time, and then he was killed. Sharp says he mentioned it to Harrison before the coroner's inquest, because he felt it had a bearing on Jamie's death. Harrison chose to ignore the information, and so it was never fully investigated.' She tapped the whiteboard with the end of her pen. 'These two people are now the focus of our investigation. All three men served with the Royal Logistic Corps. Carl Ashton was present with Jamie when a container load of spare parts from Afghanistan was opened. Half a kilo of cocaine was discovered in the empty fuel tank from one of the four-by-four vehicles that the army use in Afghanistan.'

'Jesus,' said Gavin. 'What was the street value of that ten years ago?'

'Lots,' said Barnes, and gestured to Kay to carry on.

'Sharp confirmed the find occurred after Jamie's fifth tour in Afghanistan. The time before that, he bought his motorbike – a top of the range model that he shouldn't have been able to afford on a soldier's wage. In addition, the barmaid at the local pub was sporting a new pair of diamond earrings.'

'So, you're saying that Jamie was smuggling cocaine into the country within the spare parts?' said Gavin.

'Exactly, but he must have had help. It would have been too risky to plant the drugs at the base in Afghanistan, and then ensure the container got through customs without a hitch before being opened at the barracks in England. Carterton provided another name – Glenn Boyd. We need to interview them both now as a priority.'

'Will we be able to, given that they're army?' said Carys.

'Both were demobbed within six months of Jamie's death, and both live in the area. That means we have jurisdiction.'

'What were their roles at the time?' said Barnes.

'Ashton was a private. Boyd was Stephen Carterton's adjutant at the time. Jamie would've needed someone higher up to protect the operation, and Sharp suspects there was something going on between him and the adjutant prior to the drugs being found.'

'Based on what evidence?'

'Apparently, six months before the drugs were discovered, Jamie was back at the barracks in Surrey and Sharp found Boyd beating the crap out of him one night behind the depot. He and his RMPs had to break it up. They were lucky, apparently – no charges were laid.'

'What happened there, then, I wonder?' said Barnes.

'It was put down to personal differences at the time,' said Kay. 'Sharp said they thought Jamie had become arrogant over the course of that year, so maybe Boyd felt he needed pulling into line. It wasn't until afterwards that Sharp wondered if there was more to it.'

'Have we got addresses for them?'

'Yes. When personnel leave the army, they are still regarded as reservists for twenty years, so the army has up-to-date details for them at all times. I spoke with Carterton this morning, and he got the records for me.' She placed the pen on the desk, then leaned against it. 'What availability can you give me to go and interview these two?'

'I'm clear now that the court case is out of the way,' said Barnes. 'I've got some bits and pieces to clear up, but nothing urgent.'

'I can't,' said Carys. She jerked her thumb over her shoulder. 'I got back yesterday to a heap of emails, and one of my burglary cases is being reviewed by the Crown Prosecution Service later this afternoon.'

Gavin held up his hand. 'Count me in. I can help with one of them.'

'Okay, great. I'll set up the two interviews, and I'll let you have the details later today. Carys – if you need me to review anything about that case of yours, you'd best let me have that within the hour, as I might not be available tomorrow.'

'Thanks, will do.'

'Right, then we'll look at having a further briefing tomorrow night. That'll have to do for today – I've got a meeting to go to. Barnes, Gavin – I'll ask Debbie to set up the interviews and confirm with us in due course. Keep an eye on your emails and text messages.'

She watched them file from the room, and then set her shoulders.

The next meeting would take all her wits, and she hoped she was prepared.

EIGHTEEN

'Kay, good to see you. Take a seat.'

Kay closed the door and appraised the woman standing behind a desk, who offered an outstretched hand.

The practice was run from Dr Zoe Strathmore's home, and accessed through a separate entrance to the main front door for the property, ensuring privacy for her clients. The consulting room maintained a homely atmosphere, however, and as Kay took a seat in front of the desk in a stylish and comfortable armchair, Strathmore made her way to an expensive-looking coffee machine and raised an eyebrow.

'Can I tempt you? The French roast is particularly good, although I may be biased.'

Kay smiled. 'In that case, yes I can be tempted.'

'Great. I don't usually drink coffee in the afternoons, so I can use you as my excuse.'

Strathmore laughed, a pretty sound that filled the small space, and Kay felt her shoulders relax as she glanced around at her surroundings.

She had never been to a psychiatrist before, even during the emotional turmoil of the past two years. She'd never really understood the point. If something was bothering her, she simply talked to Adam about it, and vice versa.

If she was honest with herself, the prospect of the meeting had made her nervous, but Strathmore's friendly demeanour and the non-clinical decor of the surroundings began to calm her nerves.

Strathmore returned to the desk, set down two mugs of steaming coffee, and pushed the sugar bowl towards Kay.

'Help yourself if you need it.'

'Thanks.'

'Right, well, why don't we begin with me telling you about this process, and then we'll have a chat, and if you have any questions afterwards, then ask away. How does that sound?'

Kay shrugged, then took a sip of coffee as she gathered her thoughts. 'Okay, I suppose.'

Strathmore clasped her hands together on the

desk. 'I can imagine like many of your colleagues who I've met with before, part of you is thinking this is a waste of time, and the other part of you is intrigued. In your case, you've only been assigned this one session, which means that your management team are confident that you're making a full recovery, and that you are more than capable of carrying out your duties. My role is to make sure that they haven't misunderstood any signals you've been unconsciously giving them, and that you feel that you're ready to take on a frontline role once more.'

'I am.'

'Good,' said Strathmore. She gestured at the closed file at her elbow. 'I read what happened to you before Christmas. Do you mind taking me through it in your own words?'

Kay sighed. She placed her half empty coffee mug on the desk. 'I suppose if I don't, then it will go on my file, right?'

'Not at all. Your appointment, and everything we discuss here today, is confidential. My report to your management will only confirm your attendance, and whether or not I think you're capable of carrying out your duties. It's a process, that's all. So, do you want to take me through the events of the last few days of the Demiri case?'

A chill stretched its fingers across Kay's shoulders, and she fought down the urge to shudder.

She had never discussed the events of that night with anyone except the two senior officers tasked with interviewing her while she was recovering in hospital. Even Adam hadn't heard the full story – she didn't want to upset him, in case he tried to persuade her to leave the police force.

Now, a complete stranger was asking her to delve into her darkest memories.

'Kay?'

She blinked. 'There's not a lot to tell. I was set up. A senior officer turned out to be more determined than I was to arrest Demiri, and I got caught in the crossfire.'

Strathmore tilted her head. 'So, you were betrayed by one of your own?'

'Yeah. And, before you asked me how that made me feel, I was bloody angry about it when I found out.'

'Are you still angry?'

'Yes, I am. It's been months since it happened, and they're still investigating him. I mean, there were enough of us around at the time that saw what happened, and how he screwed all of us over. I don't understand what's taking them so long.'

'What happened when you and Demiri were alone on the beach?'

'He tried to kill me. I was stupid – I fell straight into the trap. I believed information I was given by someone who turned out to be working for him. I sent my colleague back for reinforcements, and instead of waiting I went on without him. Demiri was waiting for me, and attacked me. He broke my arm, two ribs, and then tried to drown me.'

'And yet, you applied to return to work a whole month earlier than you were due.'

'I had to. I was going up the wall at home. I needed to get out, and get back to work.'

'Your husband, Adam. Did he mind you returning to work early?'

Kay shook her head. 'No – he knows what I'm like. We both decided it was best if I cut short my time off.'

'Were you having nightmares?'

'No.'

'It's okay to tell me if you were, or still are.'

'No, no nightmares.'

'How have you found being back at work?'

'The first few days were dreadful – I was so bored.' Kay choked out a laugh. 'I've managed to find a cold case to get my teeth into. That's helping.

Hopefully if I get a result on this, they'll put me back on full duties.'

She reached out and picked up her coffee before frowning, surprised that it had grown cold. She checked her watch, and saw that a whole half an hour had passed.

Strathmore smiled. 'It goes a lot quicker than you think it will.'

'It did. What happens next?'

'Well, I'll complete my report and I'll email it over to your personnel team before the end of the week. In the meantime,' she said, slipping a business card across the desk towards Kay, 'take that with you, and if you ever feel that you need to talk to someone in confidence about what happened to you in more detail than we've done today, or you start getting nightmares, then call me. You're an extremely brave police officer, Kay, but we all have our breaking points.'

Kay pocketed the card, and rose from her seat. 'I'll remember that, thank you.'

Strathmore walked around her desk, and opened the door. She held out her hand once more as Kay passed.

'Look after yourself, Kay.'

'Thanks.'

Kay shifted her handbag on her shoulder, then pushed her way out of the side door from the house, and hurried over to her car.

She sat behind the wheel for a moment, her hands shaking as she gulped in a great lungful of air. Sweat prickled at the base of her skull, and she dug her fingernails into the soft skin of her palms.

She caught a movement out of the corner of her eye, and noticed the blinds at Strathmore's office window twitch back into place.

'Shit.'

She blinked to clear the tears that threatened, turned the key in the ignition, and steered the car out of the short driveway and onto the main road.

Right now, all she wanted was to be home.

NINETEEN

Kay inserted her key into the lock and pushed the door open, exhaustion seizing hold of her the moment it was shut behind her.

She hung her coat over the banister, dropped her bag onto the bottom stair tread, and slipped off her shoes before padding through to the kitchen.

'How did it go?'

Adam stood at the stove, two pots bubbling on the hob that sent Kay's taste buds into overdrive.

She wandered across and wrapped her arms around him, gave him a kiss, and then sank into his embrace.

'That good, huh?'

'I don't know whether I'm more overwhelmed by going back to work, this cold case investigation, or having to keep repeating to people that I'm okay and that I can do my job.'

'What did the psychiatrist have to say?'

Despite herself, Kay smiled and raised her eyes to his. 'Not a lot. The idea is for me to do the talking in those sessions. She just listens.'

He laughed. 'In that case, I'm surprised you weren't home an hour ago. What on earth did you talk about?'

'She made me tell her what happened last year. On the beach.'

His eyes darkened as he pulled away from her. 'Are you okay?'

'I suppose so. I'm trying to put it behind me, but every time I feel I'm moving on, someone else brings it up and I have to start thinking about it all over again.' She shrugged. 'I suppose it'll take time.'

'Did you tell her about the nightmares?'

Kay bit her lip.

'You didn't. Was that wise?'

Kay reached out for him, wrapping her fingers around his arm. 'I want it to be like it was, Adam. I'll get through this, I promise I will. But not with a psychiatrist. We manage all right together, you and me. Let's keep it like that, okay?'

He pressed his lips against hers, and then squeezed her hand. 'If you change your mind, if you feel like you're struggling, then say something. Promise me?'

'I promise.'

'Good. Now, go and get into a pair of jeans. I'm dishing up in twenty minutes.'

She grinned, turned on her heel, and hurried upstairs to change.

As she pulled off her work clothes and slipped on her jeans and a long-sleeved T-shirt, she eyed the sleeping pills on her bedside table.

She had drawn the line at taking any prescription medication, but had agreed with Adam to try a natural remedy to see if they would help ward off the nightmares that had plagued her for the past three months. She couldn't afford for her colleagues to think she couldn't do her job – as it was, the nightmares were sporadic, and so she didn't want a record of them on her medical notes.

Once the plaster cast had been removed from her arm, and she'd been given the all clear by her physiotherapist, she had returned to her running routine. Only six weeks in, and she could already sense that the exercise was helping to reduce the nightmares anyway.

She sure as hell wasn't going to tell the psychiatrist about them.

She wandered back downstairs, and seeing Adam was busy at the stove, she wandered over to Rufus, crouched down, and scratched him behind his ears.

'And how is this one doing today?'

Adam glanced over his shoulder. 'He's perked up a bit, actually. I've cooked some extra vegetables for him to have tonight, and he can have some of this roast lamb.'

The dog's brown eyes widened, and Kay laughed.

'He heard that.'

'Yeah, his foster carer, Graham, said he doesn't have a problem understanding any words that mention food. I'm finding out he's got quite a good vocabulary.'

Kay straightened, and moved to the sink to wash her hands. 'I take it, then, that his continuing education has included a lot of free food this week?'

Adam shrugged, before lowering his voice. 'I don't know how long he's got, Kay. I don't mind spoiling him.'

She wandered over, and patted his arm. 'I know. Nothing wrong with that.'

She turned and pulled out a drawer, selecting cutlery and a carving knife for Adam, before setting it on the worktop. Next, she let her eyes wander over the selection in the wine rack, then chose a Shiraz, and poured two generous measures.

'Perfect timing,' said Adam, and began to serve their food.

Once they were seated, they ate in silence for a while, until Adam pushed back his plate, and belched.

'Charmer.'

A moment later, a similar noise erupted from Rufus's corner of the room, and they laughed.

'That's ma boy,' said Adam. He patted his stomach. 'That was good, even though I do say so myself. How is that cold case of yours coming along?'

'We continue interviewing tomorrow. We've spoken to the family, as well as the victim's old commanding officer in the army. I think Sharp is right – I think there's more to this than a motorbike accident.'

'So, Harrison did cover up something?'

'Absolutely.'

'When can you take this to Larch? Won't he want to know as soon as possible if Harrison was responsible?'

Kay shook her head. 'It's not as simple as that. There's no point in my taking it to Larch now, only for our investigation to then find out that it really was an accident. I need to look at every angle again, and then we're going to have to put together enough evidence to prove that Jamie was murdered before the Crown Prosecution Service will look at it. I want to give Larch as much ammunition as possible against Harrison.'

'It must be hard for the family, having this all dragged up again after ten years.'

'I know. That's why I want to make sure we do this right, so we don't let them down.'

TWENTY

The next morning, Kay stared out of the passenger window of the car, lost in thought as she cradled her arm in her lap.

'Does it still hurt?'

'Hmm?'

She turned back to Barnes, who glanced across at her, then back at the road.

'Does your arm hurt? You've been holding it like that since we left Maidstone.'

'It aches sometimes, rather than hurts. I guess I just find it comfortable sitting like this. I got used to it over three months.'

He smiled. 'Glad you bounced back, Hunter. It's not been the same without you around.'

'Thanks, Ian.'

'Yeah. I had to make my own tea, buy my own pens—'

She laughed, and slapped his arm. 'Idiot.'

'What was the meeting about yesterday, if it's all right to ask? You seemed preoccupied when you came in this morning.'

She shrugged. She knew Barnes wouldn't gossip.

'Occupational health assessment at the end of February recommended I speak with a psychiatrist when I got back to work.'

'You okay? Not having nightmares or anything?'

'It was more of a precaution, rather than anything else. Probably for their benefit rather than mine. Jozef Demiri is dead. He can't hurt me anymore, and to be honest, Ian, I was going up the wall with boredom at home.'

'Surely not.'

'Stop it,' she said, and grinned. She pointed out of the windscreen. 'You might want to take this junction. I heard on the news this morning there were delays at the next one because of roadworks.'

'Will do.'

Kay leaned over and rummaged in her bag for her notes as Barnes eased the car off the motorway and set them on course for Faversham town centre.

'Seems sort of ironic we're in East Division's

territory given Harrison's involvement last year. Bandit country.'

'Don't worry. Larch cleared it for us. In the circumstances, once he dropped the chief super's name into the conversation, they couldn't really say no. We'll keep them informed if anything comes out of this, don't worry.'

Twenty minutes later, Barnes applied the handbrake and climbed from the car.

When Kay returned from the ticket machine, he was tapping his fingers on the roof of the vehicle.

'How do you want to do this?'

Kay handed him the ticket, and adjusted her bag over her shoulder. 'Carefully, because if he was party to smuggling drugs into the country with Jamie, I don't want a criminal defence solicitor getting him out of it because we didn't do our jobs properly. For now, he's a witness, nothing more.'

'You mean, see what he says and then decide whether to bring him in for formal questioning?'

'Exactly.'

Barnes nodded, then locked the car and led the way across the road and along a footpath that separated a pub garden and another property.

They emerged in a pedestrianised street, the

mediaeval layout of the market town still evident in the uneven surface of the lanes.

'Good cop, bad cop?'

Kay smiled, and held out her fist before flicking out two fingers.

Barnes's hand remained in a tight grip. 'You're the good cop, then. Come on – the bar he owns is down the street here.'

They entered a narrow lane that ended in a dead end, with a travel agent and a betting shop on one side, and the wine bar on the other.

A signboard hung above the door in the style of an old English pub, yet the exterior denoted a modern establishment that appeared to be doing a roaring trade despite the early hour of the day.

Barnes pushed through the door, holding it open for Kay.

As her eyes adjusted to the low light levels, she noticed a woman standing behind the bar at the far end and began to weave her way between the tables.

As well as being a wine bar, it seemed Carl Ashton's premises also offered coffee and other hot drinks, as most of the tables were taken up by what appeared to be tourists rather than locals.

Kay noticed that the few locals that were in at this

time preferred to sit at the bar, away from the strangers.

She moved to the end of a set of six beer pumps, and after showing her warrant card, asked to see Ashton.

'He's upstairs in the office,' said the woman. She cast her eyes over the throng, as if to make sure everything was under control, and then turned back to Kay. 'I'll go and get him for you. Hang on.'

Barnes leaned against a coin-operated cigarette machine, and retrieved his notebook from his jacket. Moments later, he jerked his chin over Kay's shoulder.

Ashton was the same height as Barnes, except his shoulders were broader and his stomach held a paunch no doubt aided by his current occupation. His mousy brown hair was beginning to thin, and she noticed his fingernails were chewed to the quick.

His eyes darted from her to Barnes, and then he stuck out his hand.

'Detectives? How can I help you?'

'Is there somewhere we can talk in private?' said Kay, ignoring the offered hand.

He glanced over his shoulder at the woman behind the bar, and then gestured to them to follow him. 'We can use the office. It's cramped, but it will have to do. We can't use the kitchen – I've got a gas fitter here fixing one of the chip fryers.'

He led the way through a door at the back of the bar, before turning left and climbing a narrow staircase.

At the top step, he turned right and pushed open a door. 'In you go.'

Kay nodded her thanks as she passed, then shrank back as she entered the room.

Ashton wasn't joking – the office contained a desk, a moth-eaten chair, and not much else.

'Hang on. I've got a couple of camping chairs you can sit on.'

She waited while he unfolded a chair that had been stored behind the door, and then took a seat while he did the same for Barnes.

That done, he closed the windows that were open on the computer screen, then turned to her and Barnes, and smiled. 'Now, what did you want to speak to me about? I don't recall phoning the police about anything – it's been months since the last break in.'

Kay held up her warrant card, and waited until Barnes had done likewise before formally introducing them.

'Mr Ashton, we're here to talk to you about Jamie

Ingram.' She recited the formal caution before continuing, noticing the man's posture stiffen. 'My team and I have reopened the investigation into Jamie's death, and I understand at the time you were serving with him in the Royal Logistics Corps.'

Ashton ran a hand over his mouth and then leaned his elbow on the desk. 'That's right. Crumbs, it seems like a lifetime ago.'

Kay cast her gaze around the small room, and at the photographs on the wall depicting Ashton with various minor celebrities from the area. 'You have a nice place, here. How did you manage to afford to set it up on an army salary?'

'I received an inheritance a few months before being demobbed. Came in handy, I can tell you. You're right – I wouldn't have been able to establish the business on what I earned in the army.'

'It must be hard work, running a place like this. Do you enjoy it?'

She watched as he puffed out his chest and sat up straighter.

'Well, it's not easy, this business, you know. It's long hours, and I'm constantly having to ensure my staff keep up the high standards I insist on maintaining. We have a good regular clientele, though, and since I took the initiative and provided a café-style bistro service on weekdays, I'm seeing good returns.' He tapped the side of his nose. 'It's my experience, you see. I've watched a lot of competitors come and go over the years, but they can't match my entrepreneurial skills.'

'What was your role in the Corps?'

'I was a private. Same as Jamie. We enlisted a week apart from each other, but then ended up being posted together at Deepcut. When we found out we were both from Kent, we became friends.'

'Did you socialise with him much outside of the army?'

Ashton smiled. 'Yeah. We used to have a right laugh off barracks. His parents own a fruit farm outside Maidstone – plums, apples and stuff like that. Jamie was into his motorbikes like me, so we used to spend time tearing along the tracks around the property in the summer.'

'So, you knew his family well?'

'Sort of, I guess. His sister was a looker, I remember that. His mum was German, right?'

'Correct.' Kay took a moment to run her gaze over her notes, even though she knew them by rote. Often, witness interviews were about pacing, and it wouldn't do to rush her questions. 'Were you also posted in Afghanistan with Jamie?'

'Yes. Every single time. We were in the same unit, see?'

'What did your role entail?'

He leaned back. 'Well, when we were in Afghanistan we were responsible for making sure the equipment was fit for purpose. If anything was broken, we either got the Royal Electrical and Mechanical Engineers involved if it was a mechanical issue, or we arranged for spare parts to be shipped out to us. We'd crate up anything that we couldn't fix there and arrange for it to be sent back to the UK.'

Kay remained silent.

'Is that how Jamie managed to smuggle the cocaine into the country?' said Barnes.

'What?' Ashton's elbow slipped off the desk, throwing him off balance. He recovered, and glared at Barnes, his face ashen.

'Tell us about the half kilo of cocaine that was discovered in an empty fuel tank from a Jackal,' said Kay. 'How did it get there?'

'I have no idea.'

'You must've been relieved when Jamie died and the investigation was dropped,' said Barnes. 'Rather convenient for you, wasn't it?'

Ashton rose from his seat, the wheels sending it crashing into the wall behind him. 'Now, hang on.

You can't walk in here and start accusing me of killing Jamie!'

'I don't believe my colleague stated that,' said Kay, keeping her voice calm. 'So, sit down.'

Ashton glared at her, but she held his gaze until he sank back into his chair, his hands shaking. 'You know what? Instead of coming in here, talking about drug smuggling and suggesting I murdered my best mate, why don't you speak to Glenn Boyd?'

'The adjutant?'

He sneered. 'Yeah, him. Jamie was having an affair with his wife, after all. I'd say that's a pretty good motive for wanting him out of the way, wouldn't you?'

Kay rose from her chair. 'Thank you, Mr Ashton. I think that will do for now. We'll be in touch.'

She waited until she and Barnes were outside, and then turned to him as the door to the bar closed behind them.

'What do you think?'

'He's either lying through his teeth, or he's running a dodgy business. Either way, I think the next interview with him will involve a solicitor.'

Kay pursed her lips. 'My thoughts exactly.'

TWENTY-ONE

Back at the incident room, Kay pushed her computer keyboard aside, then peered at Barnes.

'How did we not know Jamie Ingram was having an affair with the adjutant's wife?'

He paused as he walked past, then shuffled a bundle of papers before dropping them onto his chair and reaching over the back of it for a mug of tea.

'Because no-one volunteered that nugget of information the first time around, or they did and Harrison chose to ignore it.' He took a swig, then grimaced. 'Debbie? Tea's cold.'

'That's what happens when you ignore it for half an hour after I shoved it under your nose.'

'Any chance of a—'

'Make it yourself. I've got Carl Ashton's witness

statement to type up, and your writing's atrocious. You should take some typing lessons, you know. It'd save me a lot of headaches.'

'I'm too old to learn anything new, Debs.'

'Dinosaur.'

Kay ignored the banter between her colleagues, and instead turned her attention back to the HOLMES database.

'Was the adjutant interviewed at the time?' said Barnes.

'Yeah, on the basis that he was the one Jamie had to go through to request a meeting with his commanding officer.'

'And I suppose it was only Sharp's assumption that the adjutant had something to do with the supply of drugs, because it needed someone high up to sign off the paperwork when the containers arrived back in the UK?'

'Right. Because it was so tenuous, Sharp's boss in the Royal Military Police didn't mention it to Kent Police at the time, so Glenn Boyd wasn't formally interviewed about that. They only approached him to check out Jamie's movements in the days leading up to his death. Let's face it; Kent Police didn't have any cause to suspect foul play at the time because

Harrison had suppressed the information Sharp gave him.'

'Jamie Ingram was a bit of a dark horse, wasn't he?' said Gavin as he wandered over from his desk and handed Kay a single sheet of paper. 'These are the details for Mrs Boyd that Debbie dug out. Seems she and Glenn are still married, so I don't know if her affair with Jamie was ever mentioned.'

'Thanks, Gavin. Can you join me to interview her tomorrow?'

'Sure – there's a landline number for the property, so I'll give her a call now.'

'Tread carefully when you do. No point in dragging up the subject of the affair in front of her husband.'

'Noted. How would you describe Ashton when you spoke with him?'

'A braggart.'

'Kay's being polite,' said Barnes. 'What she means is, he could talk the hind leg off a donkey.'

Kay smiled. 'Yeah, he certainly fancied himself as a man about town, that's for sure.' She paused, and twisted in her seat. 'Debbie? When you have time tomorrow, could you take a closer look at the history for Ashton's bar? Right back to when he first purchased it.'

'Will do.'

'Also, any licensing infringements, police involvement, that sort of thing. He mentioned a break-in a few months ago, so there's probably something on the system about that.'

'You still think he used the drugs to pay for the business?' said Barnes.

'Yes, I do. And I want to know if he's continued to deal. I mean, you've seen the statistics in the news – pubs were struggling before the recession, and it hasn't improved much since.'

'What about his accusation regarding Jamie and the adjutant's wife, then? Do you think there's some truth in that, or is he telling us that as a way to send us off on a fool's errand?'

'I'm sure he's using it for deflection, yes.'

She turned to Gavin. 'Can you do me a favour? Can you look into Glenn and Penny Boyd's background and check to see if there are any offences on the database in relation to either of them?'

'Will do. I might not have that for you before we speak to them, though.' He jerked his thumb over his shoulder. 'I've just had a car theft job land on my desk, but I'll do my best.'

'Great, thanks.'

Barnes pushed away from the wall and crossed his arms. 'All right. Now what?'

Kay stretched her hands above her head with a groan, then cricked her neck.

'Pub. First round's on me.'

TWENTY-TWO

The next morning, Kay sat in the passenger seat of the oldest pool car they had found in the car park, and blew on her fingers.

Steam rose from two Styrofoam cups of coffee that had been placed in the holders between the seats, and Gavin leaned over the steering wheel to wipe away the condensation that had formed on the windscreen.

'Remind me again why we picked the car with no heating? This thing is a heap of rust – the gearbox is falling apart, and I'm sure the handbrake is going to give way at any time.'

'Yes, but it doesn't look like a police car, either. Much easier for us to go unnoticed.'

She raised her chin as a door opened at a house

further along the street, and a man hurried along the garden path and through a gate, before unlocking a blue hatchback car.

'There he goes.'

They turned their attention away from the car as it passed their vehicle, arguing in case the driver glanced their way, and then dropping the pretence the moment he was out of sight.

Kay turned in her seat and watched through the back window as the car indicated right and joined the flow of traffic on the main road heading towards Maidstone town centre.

'Where did you say he worked?'

'At a firm of solicitors. He studied for a law degree while he was in the army, and pursued a career with one of the local firms after he was demobbed.'

She checked her watch. 'Okay, we've got half an hour before she's due to go to work.'

They climbed from the vehicle, and made their way along the narrow pavement towards the house. The door opened the moment their feet began to crunch on the gravel path leading to it.

A woman peered out at them, concern in her eyes.

'Mrs Penny Boyd? I'm DI Kay Hunter. You spoke to my colleague here, DC Gavin Piper, yesterday. We'd like to talk to you about Jamie Ingram.'

Penny beckoned to them. 'Hurry up. Before the neighbours see you.'

Kay wiped her feet on the doormat, and stepped over the threshold into a hallway. She shuffled along to make room for Gavin, and waited while the woman slammed the door shut.

She turned to Kay and Gavin, her dark eyebrows a striking contrast against her pale blonde bob hairstyle, and played with a single silver chain at her neck. She wore a business suit, and was clearly agitated.

'I've got to get to work. I really don't have time for this.'

'Can we sit down somewhere?'

The woman's fingers fluttered away from the necklace, and she pointed a shaking hand over Kay's shoulder. 'Living room's through there.'

'Thanks.'

Kay waited until Penny led the way, and then followed her into a bright room that overlooked the street.

Net curtains obscured the neighbours' view of the room, and a sofa had been placed beneath the windowsill, facing a large television on the opposite wall. Two armchairs were against the far wall, and it was to these that Penny gestured.

'Take a seat.'

Gavin pulled his notebook from his jacket pocket as Penny lowered herself onto the sofa and curled up her legs underneath her.

'When you phoned, I thought it was about the break-in further up the street last week.'

'What was that?'

Penny gave a dismissive wave of her hand. 'Oh, kids, I expect. One of our neighbours' cars had its window smashed and a tablet computer taken off the seat.' She rolled her eyes. 'As if you lot don't warn people enough about that.'

Kay gave her a small smile. 'No, we'd like to talk to you about Jamie.'

'I haven't thought about him in years.'

'How well did you know him?'

Penny's eyes narrowed. 'Well, if you're here about Jamie, you could've only heard it from one person. Carl Ashton, right?'

'I'm afraid I can't divulge my sources, Mrs Boyd.'

The woman snorted. 'Of course not. Even if he's trying to ruin my marriage.'

'How did you and Jamie meet?'

'At a party, the first time they all came back from Afghanistan. God, I can't tell you the relief. I don't miss those days at all. Six months of boredom mixed with an unhealthy dose of terror every time they left. I hated it.'

'What happened?'

'I had too much to drink, Detective. Isn't that usually the way these things happen?'

'I wouldn't know. Was that the only time?'

Penny lowered her gaze to her lap and picked at an imaginary piece of lint on her trousers. 'No.'

'Tell me.'

'We saw each other quite a bit. When he wasn't out of the country, I mean.' Penny reached out and plucked two paper tissues from the box on the coffee table, before dabbing at her eyes. 'I blamed myself for his death, you know. I didn't kill him, of course, but I may as well have, after everything that happened.'

Kay caught Gavin's quizzical glance her way, and then turned her attention back to Penny.

'I'm sorry, Mrs Boyd. You've lost me. Can you explain that statement?'

The woman clenched the sodden tissues in her palm, her face distraught.

'The police never asked me, you see. Not yours, or ours – I mean, the army. I tried to convince myself it wasn't my fault.'

She gasped then, a deep sucking breath that made her shoulders heave. 'Excuse me.'

Gavin went to rise from his seat as Penny launched herself from the sofa and hurried from the room, but Kay shook her head.

'It's okay. Give her a moment.'

The sound of retching reached Kay's ears, and Gavin's face registered understanding.

A while later, Penny returned, a glass of water in her hand and her cheeks flushed.

'I'm so sorry.'

She moved to the sofa once more, took a sip of water, and set the glass next to the box of tissues.

'Mrs Boyd? What happened?' said Kay.

The woman took a deep, shuddering breath.

'It's my fault he died that night,' she said. 'We'd argued, you see. I phoned him while he was at the farm. It was in the evening – I think he and his parents had already finished dinner, and he made me wait while he got out of the house to talk to me.'

'What did you argue about?'

Penny's jaw set. 'I wanted to break it off. Our affair. It was becoming too intense. I—' She paused to blow her nose. 'Look, for me, it was a bit of fun, that's all. Jamie was good-looking, he was up for it. I don't know. It was exciting.'

A hint of petulance peppered the last words, and Kay felt herself losing sympathy with the woman.

'Why is it your fault that Jamie died?'

'You see, Jamie was so angry with me. He didn't want to stop our affair. That's why he left the farm so late that night. He was coming to see me. He was going to beg me to change my mind.'

'Mrs Boyd, do you have any evidence to support that assertion?'

'No, of course not. But he was obsessed with me. It's the sort of thing he would've done in the circumstances.'

Kay exhaled, and took a moment to gather her thoughts before continuing. 'What does your husband do at the legal firm?'

'He's a partner now. His team run the accident claims department – a lot of their clients are motor vehicle insurers.'

Kay caught Gavin's gaze.

'Thank you for your time, Mrs Boyd. We'll be in touch if we need to discuss anything further.'

Penny uncurled herself from the sofa, and led them out to the front door. She stopped with her hand on the latch.

'Detective? You won't tell my husband, will you?'

'Only if the course of our investigation into Jamie's death makes it unavoidable,' said Kay.

'I haven't had another affair since Jamie,' Penny said, her tone desperate. 'I don't know. I felt that his death was God's way of punishing me for cheating on my husband.'

Kay resisted the urge to sigh.

'We'll be in touch if we have any other questions, Mrs Boyd.'

TWENTY-THREE

'What did you make of that?'

Kay read through Gavin's notes as he drove them back towards Maidstone.

'I don't think she's our suspect,' he said.

'No, I don't think so. Guilty of cheating on her husband, but that's about it. I wonder why she thinks Jamie's accident is her fault.'

'Well, like she said, if he was desperate to see her to make her reconsider breaking off their affair, maybe he wasn't concentrating hard enough on the road conditions that night.'

'Maybe.'

'Motor vehicle accidents, though? Too much of a coincidence, don't you think, that her husband works in that area of law?' Gavin nosed the car into the traffic, and held up his hand in thanks as another driver braked to let him through.

'How did that not get picked up on the system?' said Kay.

'His biography on the firm's site is only a general one, and it doesn't mention anything about motor vehicles.'

'Right, well let's see what Mr Boyd has to say for himself.'

'What about the fact his wife was having an affair?'

'I'm a detective, not a marriage wrecker,' said Kay. 'It serves no purpose bringing that up.'

She pulled her phone from her bag, and dialled the number for the firm of solicitors that Glenn Boyd now worked for. After five minutes negotiating with the receptionist, she made an appointment to meet with him later that morning.

'Right, well, we might as well go and get something to eat while we wait. If we go back to the station, we may never escape again.'

Gavin manoeuvred the car into the correct lane on the ring road to take them into the town centre.

Kay wouldn't have put money on it, but he found a parking space only metres from their favourite café and turned to her with a wide smile.

'You can wipe that smug look off your face, Piper. You're paying for breakfast.'

An hour later, they arrived at the front door to the firm of solicitors with ten minutes to spare.

Like many of the professional firms around the town, the firm was housed in a row of seventeenth-century buildings that had been knocked into one on the inside, providing ample space for the partners, associates, and administrative staff that were needed to run the business efficiently.

The refurbishment had been carried out tastefully, too.

Kay admired the exposed beams, their dark colours standing out in contrast to the pale coloured walls. She loved the way that the interior walls hadn't been straightened out by the builders. Instead, their uneven surface served as a feature in the reception area.

The receptionist waved them to two armchairs, plucking a phone from its cradle and putting it to her ear as they made themselves comfortable.

They didn't have to wait long.

A man's voice reached Kay's ears from the direction of an archway that had been left in situ behind the reception desk during the original renovations, before he stepped into view, shoving a mobile phone into his shirt pocket as he locked eyes with her.

He held out his hand as he approached.

'Detective Hunter? I'm Glenn Boyd.'

'Thanks for seeing us this morning. This is my colleague, DC Gavin Piper.'

'There's a spare meeting room we can use for the next hour. Would you like to follow me?'

He turned without waiting for an answer, and called over his shoulder as he led the way back through the archway.

'Helen? Can you send any phone calls for me through to Stephanie?'

Kay didn't hear the receptionist's response, but followed Boyd along the corridor a short way, before he turned left and held open a door for her and Gavin.

'Here we go. Unfortunately, I'm not high enough up in the firm yet to warrant my own office.'

'This will be fine,' said Kay.

'You mentioned on the phone it was about Jamie Ingram?'

'Yes. We've been requested to reopen the investigation into his death ten years ago, as we've received some new information.'

Boyd's brow furrowed as he lowered himself into

a chair opposite them. 'I'm presuming you can't tell me what information that is?'

Kay smiled. 'I'm sorry, no.'

He shrugged. 'Okay. What do you need to know?'

'I'd like to know where you were on the night Jamie Ingram died.'

His eyes darted from her to Gavin, and back. 'What? Am I a suspect, or something? Jamie's motorbike accident was just that – an accident, wasn't it?'

'Answer the question, please.'

'I was in the office at the barracks. All personnel were due back by midnight the next day, and you wouldn't believe the paperwork involved in getting them ready for redeployment. I had my hands full – it was one o'clock in the morning by the time I finished and went back to my quarters.'

'Do you have an alibi for that time?'

'I don't need one. The offices at the barracks had a security system that we time coded. You can pull the records, and see for yourself.'

'You must have been relieved when his crash was ruled an accident.'

'I didn't kill him, Detective.'

'You certainly had motive. You were caught

fighting with him behind the barracks six months before his death. What was all that about?'

Boyd snorted, and shook his head. A sadness filled his eyes, and he reached into his trouser pocket and pulled out a handkerchief before blowing his nose.

'Detective, you asked me just now if I had an alibi for the night Jamie died. I do, but please – be careful with this information.'

He reached out for a complimentary pen and notepad that had been set next to the water glasses in the middle of the table, and proceeded to write out a name and phone number on it. He handed it to Kay.

'I don't know if this number will still work. It's from ten years ago, after all.'

Kay bit her lip as she read the text, and then raised her gaze to meet his.

'You see,' he said, 'my wife wasn't the only one having an affair. I'm sure you'll find out about her and Jamie Ingram during the course of your enquiries. Life in the army is hard. You find yourself drifting away from those you love the most.'

'And yet, you're both still together.'

'She never found out about my affair. She thinks I didn't know about her and Jamie. I love her. I always will.'

Kay sighed, and passed the piece of paper to Gavin, who tucked it into his notebook. She turned back to Boyd.

'Tell me about the drugs. How were they getting into the country?'

'Did Devon Sharp or Stephen Carterton tell you about the empty fuel tank?'

'I'm not at liberty to say who told us.'

'Well, it was hardly a secret once half a kilo of cocaine was found. We never did find out how they managed it. More's the pity. Then Jamie died, and the investigation petered out.'

'Did Jamie seem scared in the days leading up to his death?'

Boyd stared into space for a moment, then blinked. 'Not scared, no. Distracted, yes. As if there was something on his mind. At the time, I thought it might have been linked to the drugs that were found, but I'm not sure now.'

'Surely imported goods would've needed someone higher up to sign off the paperwork? Jamie must've had help higher up to pull off that amount of smuggling.'

Boyd shook his head. 'Not me, and I don't believe Carterton would have done, either – not the way he ripped the place apart when those drugs were found.

It was his reputation on the line, not to mention the criminal prosecutions that would hang over the regiment. He'd never risk it.'

'So, who?'

He loosened his tie before resting his elbows on the table. 'There was a captain who used to work in the office at the barracks – procurement and the like. I had my doubts about him, to be honest, but it's too late now.'

'Why?'

'He died two years ago after a massive stroke, Detective.'

Kay pursed her lips and fought down her frustration. 'What about the buyer? Any ideas who Jamie might have been planning to sell the drugs to?'

'I'm sorry, no.'

TWENTY-FOUR

Kay tapped her pen against the desk, wondering which angle of enquiry she could pursue next, before she tossed it onto a pile of folders and strode into Sharp's office.

Carys joined her as she paced in front of the whiteboard.

'You usually moan at Sharp for wearing out the carpet.'

'I'm beginning to understand why he does this.'

'Penny for your thoughts?'

'I'm not sure they're worth that at the moment.'

'Try me.' Carys sank into one of the visitor chairs next to Sharp's desk and then glanced up as Gavin, Debbie, and Barnes joined them. 'Good timing.'

'I've got those records and everything you requested about Carl Ashton's wine bar,' said Debbie, handing over a folder to Kay. 'And I made copies for everyone else.'

'Cheers, thanks. Great work.'

Barnes swore under his breath as he leaned against the windowsill and turned the pages. 'This business should have gone under two years ago.'

'We're either right, and he's using cash to prop up the business, or he's got a very clever accountant,' said Kay as she ran her gaze over the news clippings depicting extravagant refurbishments and charity donations.

'When was the bar established?' said Barnes.

'Nine years ago,' said Debbie. 'He registered the business as a public limited company two years ago. We'll obviously need a warrant for his accounting records.'

'So, we might only be seeing an indication of a fraction of the money that's gone through that bar?'

'Exactly.'

'I wonder what made him register the business?' said Gavin.

Kay flicked through the pages at the end of the report, and then flung it onto Sharp's desk. 'He's protecting himself. If the business goes into liquidation, he can walk away and no-one can do anything about it.'

'Which makes you wonder if his "inheritance" is starting to run out,' said Barnes.

'Exactly. How did you get on doing the background checks on Glenn and Penny Boyd, Gavin?' said Kay.

'There's nothing of concern,' he said. 'I think they're both in the clear with regard to the drugs.'

'Do you think he knew his wife continued her affair with Jamie after he'd beaten him up that time?' said Carys.

'No, I don't,' said Kay. 'Mind you, it's hard to have any sympathy for either of them – they're as bad as each other in that respect.'

'So, back to what we were saying. What do you think was going on?'

'Okay, this is what we know so far. Jamie and, possibly, Ashton was smuggling cocaine into the country, using equipment coming back from Afghanistan to hide it in. Glenn Boyd said that the senior officer responsible for signing off that equipment for Customs and Excise purposes died of a stroke two years ago, so we can't interview him. There wasn't enough evidence at the time to charge

Jamie, but an investigation by the Royal Military Police was underway when he died.'

'Do you think someone killed him to silence him, then?'

'I'm not sure. I mean – why kill someone who was your only supply source?'

'Rivalry? Perhaps somebody else had a vested interest in smuggling the drugs into the country?' said Barnes.

Kay scribbled the suggestion on the whiteboard. 'It's worth considering. After all, half a kilo of cocaine isn't cheap. I'm sure once word got around that a few people would have been left wondering how he managed to smuggle it in.'

'Do you think he had done it before?' said Gavin.

'If he did, then how did he get away with it?'

'Luck, perhaps.' Gavin shrugged. 'Sometimes, that's all it takes. Did Stephen Carterton say that they checked every container that came back, or did they pick one or two at random?'

'He didn't,' said Kay. 'Carys – can you clarify that with him?'

'Will do. You think they were cutting corners on their Customs and Excise responsibilities?'

'Bet they didn't once they found half a kilo that time,' said Barnes. 'No wonder Sharp said they turned the barracks inside out trying to find out who smuggled it in.'

'On top of that, from everything we've gone through, we still don't know who he was supplying to. I mean, half a kilo of cocaine is an enormous amount to risk bringing in, let alone trying to distribute it. And, from what we're hearing, that wasn't the only time. So, who the hell was buying it?'

'We also have to look at the possibility of a disgruntled customer being responsible for his death,' said Barnes.

'True.' Kay added his suggestion to the board, then replaced the cap on the pen and turned to the team. 'Well, that certainly gives us some work to do.'

Barnes pushed himself away from the windowsill. 'What you want to do next?'

'Arrest Carl Ashton and bring him in for questioning in relation to the drug smuggling. Can you arrange that, Carys?'

'Will do.'

'Good. We'll do the interview first thing in the morning.'

'I'll bring the coffee,' said Barnes.

TWENTY-FIVE

The following morning, Kay opened the door to interview room two and stepped aside so that Carl Ashton and his solicitor could enter.

As they took their seats, Barnes checked the recording equipment and issued Ashton with the formal caution before taking a seat and nodding to Kay.

She opened the folder in front of her.

'To be clear, Mr Ashton, and to follow on from what my colleague has informed you and your solicitor, this is a formal interview to ask you questions in relation to alleged money laundering, the smuggling of drugs into the UK, and your involvement in the death of Jamie Ingram.'

Ashton swallowed, and paled a little.

When he didn't answer, Kay continued.

'How long have you had the bar for?'

'About nine years. Ever since I left the army.'

'What made you decide to become a licensee?'

He smirked. 'I like beer.'

Kay narrowed her eyes at him. 'Let's not start off on the wrong foot, Mr Ashton. Don't try to be clever with me. How did you finance the purchase of the wine bar?'

He shuffled in his seat and lowered his gaze. 'It was going cheap. The last owner screwed up, and was trying to get rid of it as soon as possible.'

'That's all very interesting, but answer the question. How could you afford to buy it?'

'I told you before. I got an inheritance a few months before leaving the army.'

Kay flicked through her notes. 'Who is your accountant?'

'I use a different one these days. My old accountant retired. Why?'

'There are a number of newspaper reports available online that demonstrate you've been spending a lot of money on the business over the years. For example, you undertook a massive refurbishment prior to opening the bar, and then a year later won a local business award due to the number of staff you successfully employed. On top of that, three years ago you underwent a rebranding exercise, which I would imagine wasn't cheap, in order to launch the café you established within the building. Who did you get the inheritance from?'

'I can't remember. It might have been a great-aunt, on my dad's side. I didn't know her very well.' He shrugged. 'It was a long time ago.'

'And yet, she left you enough money in her will that you could buy a struggling business and spend significant funds to turn around its fortunes, and keep it afloat.'

'It was unexpected, that's true. As for the success of the wine bar, well that's simply hard graft on my part.'

'We'll need the details of your great-aunt's solicitors.'

'I can't remember the name of them.'

'Where are they based?'

'I can't remember. Listen, I've only got two staff working at the bar today. It's Friday. That's our busiest trading day. I don't think I have time to sit here and talk with you.'

'I don't care what you think, Mr Ashton. At the moment, things aren't looking too good for you.' Kay gestured to the paperwork before her. 'You can't tell us who you inherited your money from, after saying that that was what financed the establishment of your wine bar. The few successes that have been reported in local news don't explain how you're managing to keep your business afloat, given how many of your competitors in the area are struggling or have closed down over the years. That indicates to me that you have a cash flow problem. The sort of cash flow problem that means you can't demonstrate how your business is managing to stay afloat on its own. Now, I'm inclined to believe that some of that is due to what you're skimming off the cigarette machine takings, and I'll bet that half your staff aren't on the books and are probably being paid in cash under the minimum wage. But the rest of it?'

She stopped and then turned to Barnes, who shook his head and let an expression of disbelief cloud his features.

Ashton slammed his hand on the table, his top lip curled into a snarl. 'You can't do anything about how I choose to run my business.'

'Actually, I can.' Kay leaned forward, and glared at him. 'And we'll be passing on all this paperwork to the Inland Revenue. I'm sure they'll be delighted to hear from me.'

'You bitch.'

Kay let him fume, and then changed tack. 'Let's move on to the half kilo of cocaine that was found in the Jackal's empty fuel tank ten years ago. How was Jamie getting that into the country each time? Did you and he use the same method?'

Ashton smirked.

'Yeah. By the third time, we had it down to a fine art.'

Kay raised an eyebrow as he flushed crimson and realised his error.

'Well, well. I told you, Barnes. Mr Ashton can't help crowing about his achievements. I knew he'd trip himself up one day.'

Ashton's solicitor spluttered, and rose from his seat. 'Detective, I have to insist—'

Ashton put his hand on the man's arm and shook his head, his expression resigned. He waited until the solicitor had lowered himself back into his seat, then turned his attention back to Kay.

'I was desperate, all right? I had credit card debt coming out of my ears, and my wife had divorced me. We'd only been together a couple of years, but we had a daughter, and my ex wanted maintenance payments off me. I didn't know what else to do.'

'How did you smuggle in the drugs?'

'I wasn't to know. Jamie organised all of that.'

'Who were you selling it to?'

He shook his head. 'I don't know. Jamie wouldn't tell me.'

'Why not?'

'He said the less people knew about the arrangements, the better.'

'So, he didn't trust you?'

'I didn't say that.'

'Well, it already seems to me that you have a habit of spreading rumours in order to protect your own position. Such as telling us about Penny Boyd's affair with Jamie. Did you kill Jamie because he wouldn't tell you who the supplier was?'

His eyes wide, his head swivelled from Kay to Barnes, then back. 'I told you before – I had nothing to do with his death. It was an accident, right?'

'When was the last time you spoke with Jamie?'

'About a week before he died. I think.'

'Where were you on the night of his death?'

'I was already back at the barracks. You can check the records, can't you?'

'How much more cocaine did you bring into the country after Jamie died?'

'I didn't. I told you. Jamie was the one that organised it.'

'Explain how.'

Ashton held up his hand to stop his solicitor interrupting again, then wiped at his eyes.

'Screw it. I'm done for, anyway, aren't I? They may as well hear it all.' He sniffed, then straightened in his seat as his gaze met Kay's.

'When we were in Afghanistan, an American unit was tasked with guarding the caches of drugs that were found during raids around the province, and it was decided that the safest place to keep everything they found was in one of our storage sheds, because they were blast-proof. They placed guards on the door, of course, but Jamie and I knew them in passing and it wasn't too hard to distract them. The storage shed was quite large, and it was where we kept all the spares as well as crated up anything that had to come back to the UK. When they first stored the drugs there, we had to have one of the guards accompany us while we went about our business, but over time they got complacent. They trusted us, see?'

'Go on.'

'The first time, I think Jamie just did it to see if he could get away with it for a bit of a laugh. So, I kept on talking to the guards while he made some sort of excuse about needing something from the back of the shed. When he came back, he could hardly keep the grin off his face. Then later that day, he started panicking about what he was going to do with it. It wasn't exactly as if he could take it back to them and tell them it was just a joke, could he?'

'What happened?'

'That's when he got the idea to get some more and smuggle it back. I don't know – I think the farm was struggling at the time, and maybe Jamie didn't want that in his future. Michael always said that the farm would be passed on to Jamie, and I got the impression he wanted something better than that to look forward to once he left the army. Anyway, he didn't talk about it for the rest of our deployment – we only had about four weeks to go before we returned to the UK. When we got back, we were working to process all the parts that had been containerised and shipped back so we could get them fixed or replaced, when Jamie came up to me and told me he'd found a buyer for the cocaine. I don't think I slept for two days after that, but he told me that if I kept quiet he'd give me a cut of the profit.'

'How many times did this happen?'

Ashton swallowed. 'After that first time? Every deployment until that half kilo got discovered by accident. Until Jamie got killed.'

'How much money did you receive for helping Jamie get past the guard detail in Afghanistan?'

'Fifteen thousand pounds.'

'That doesn't seem a lot to risk your army career for.'

He lifted his chin until his eyes met hers. 'Fifteen thousand pounds, every time. That half a kilo was the smallest amount he'd ever brought in. They never found the rest.'

TWENTY-SIX

Carys looked up from her desk as Kay returned to the incident room.

After leaving Barnes to arrange to have Carl Ashton moved to the holding cells, she'd been summoned to headquarters to participate in a three-hour management workshop.

She and the other delegates had spent the afternoon fighting off lethargy and boredom while they feigned interest in an overly-enthusiastic presentation on how to manage their workloads, and wondering when they could return to their desks to do exactly that.

'I managed to get hold of someone from the Crown Prosecution Service to come over here,' said Carys as she approached. 'She's in Sharp's office.'

'That's great, thanks. Gavin – anything on that lead Glenn Boyd gave us about the bloke he reckoned was helping Jamie at this end?'

The young DC swivelled round on his chair to face her.

'I spoke to the man's wife. She confirmed he died of a massive stroke two years ago. Completely unexpected, apparently – he wasn't unhealthy, and had kept up a fitness regime since leaving the army. I'm waiting on a phone call from the tax office to see what his financial situation was like before he died, in case he was receiving money from the drug dealing.'

'Okay. Let me know if you find out anything that'll help us.'

'Will do. How did you get on with Carl Ashton?'

Kay gestured towards Sharp's office as Barnes appeared, loosening his jacket. 'We're about to find out if we have enough evidence to charge him, so I'll let you know.'

Kay closed the door as she entered the room after Barnes, and was relieved to find Jude Martin reclining in the visitor's chair next to Sharp's desk.

The CPS advisor worked closely with the officers in Kent Police to ensure cases that were brought before a court were properly managed from the moment a suspect was charged.

Dressed in a light blue suit and a cream blouse, her light blonde hair fashionably short, the woman exuded confidence and authority.

'Jude – good to see you. Thanks for coming over.'

Jude rose to shake hands with them both before retaking her seat next to Sharp's desk. 'All right, Kay. Carys said you had an interesting one for me. Let's have it.'

'We've got a suspect downstairs in relation to a cold case from ten years ago we've been tasked with investigating, but it's not straightforward and I could use your advice.'

Kay proceeded to give the CPS officer an overview of the investigation to date, and the outcome of the interview she and Barnes had conducted with Carl Ashton. 'What are our options?'

'Well, there's no evidence to suggest that Ashton is currently dealing in drugs to keep his business afloat. However, we've certainly got enough to work with to speak to the Inland Revenue regarding the financing and ongoing accounts reporting for the business. They'll be interested to hear about the cash payments, for a start.'

'So, no prosecution for the historical smuggling?'

'I didn't say that. Ashton admits to taking his share of the profits from the importation of those drugs and using it to kick-start his business. That's money laundering. He might not be part of a large syndicate, but we can still charge him under a subset of the law for self-laundering those funds.'

Kay exhaled. 'Good to hear.'

'Don't worry, I'm sure we can make his life unpleasant for quite some time. I'll be in touch.' Jude smiled, rose from her chair and tapped Kay's arm with her folder.

Kay showed her out to the reception area, and then returned to Sharp's office to find Barnes staring at the whiteboard.

'So, we have Jamie's partner in crime sorted out as far as the supply is concerned,' he said. 'But still no sign of the buyer – or Jamie's murderer.'

'I know. We're missing something, Ian, and it's bugging me. Keep me posted on what Gavin finds out about that bloke's tax records, okay?'

'No problem.'

Kay sighed, and led him back out to the incident room. 'I'll ask Carys to double check everything we have on the ex-adjutant and his wife, too in case they're working together to cover something up.'

'Uh-oh.'

'What?'

He jerked his chin, his gaze moving away from hers. 'Looks like Larch wants that update now.'

She glanced over her shoulder. 'Oh, great. Perfect timing.'

'Good luck. I'll catch you on Monday morning.'

'Yeah. Thanks, Ian.'

TWENTY-SEVEN

'My office.'

Kay followed Larch as he stalked out of the incident room and along the corridor, fighting down a sense of panic.

After all, she had a result – even if it wasn't the exact one that they were hoping for.

Carl Ashton would be charged in accordance with the Crown Prosecution Service guidelines set by Jude, and at least she had solved the mystery of half the supply chain for the drugs.

She knew what the DCI was like, though.

It wouldn't be enough.

She fought down the rising panic in her chest. She had to prove that she was capable of leading a major enquiry, and she had to get Sharp's Professional Standards investigation dropped.

Larch had stopped, and held open the door to his office for her.

'Thanks, guv.'

'I've just had a meeting at headquarters with the chief superintendent,' he said. 'She's reiterated that she is expecting results before the end of the tax year in order to be able to apply for more funding for West division. That gives us a little over six weeks to get our house in order, Hunter. So, what have you got for me?'

'We'll be charging Carl Ashton with historical supply of Class A drugs, not to mention the theft of those drugs from a secure facility in Afghanistan and money laundering from the proceeds of sale. Jude Martin from the CPS is going to look into how best to do that, given that the theft happened while he was employed by the army. Ashton will also have his file passed to the Inland Revenue due to the fact that he used money generated by the sale of those drugs to fund his business, and failed to report other cash income.'

Larch wrinkled his nose. 'Not exactly the fireworks we were after, is it?'

'I realise that, guv. We still need to find the buyer,

too.'

'Any leads?'

'No. Not at the present time. It's my intention to conduct a review next week of our investigation to date, and I hope to have a way forward once I've done that.'

'You'd better have a meeting with the family, too, so they can be brought up to date before the media gets wind of Ashton being arrested.'

'I'll make an appointment to speak with them as soon as possible.'

He sighed, and tugged the tie at his neck, coiling the material around his hand before dumping it on the desk between them.

'Close the door, Hunter.'

Kay frowned, but did as she was told before returning to her seat.

'What's going on, guv?'

'What I'm about to tell you stays within these four walls, is that understood?'

'Okay, yes.'

'We need to get Sharp back here as soon as possible. There are going to be some changes happening here soon, and I have to make sure this station is left in capable hands.'

'What do you mean?'

Kay felt her heart rate ratchet up a notch.

Larch appeared uneasy, as if he didn't know what to say, his usual brusque tone missing. He took a deep breath.

'Hunter, my wife has been diagnosed with breast cancer. It's quite advanced, and to be honest, her chances aren't good.'

'Guv, I'm so sorry.'

He shook his head, as if to compose himself. 'I've spoken with the chief superintendent. I'll be taking a sabbatical, starting in a week or so. So, as you can see – I need Sharp back here before I go. The chief superintendent has agreed with me that if we can clear his name associated with those trumped up accusations Harrison's made, then he should be acting DCI in my absence.'

Kay leaned forward, and rested her elbows on her knees while she stared at the carpet.

'I don't know what to say, guv.'

He choked out a bitter laugh. 'That's got to be a first.'

'What are you going to do? I mean, what *do* you do?'

'The doctors say she has about four months, if we are lucky. The minute I leave here, I'm taking her to France for a long weekend – friends of ours have a cottage in the country, and it's one of her favourite places. I'd like her to see that again before it's too late. After that,' he shrugged, and wiped at his eyes, 'I don't know. I suppose we'll have to see how things go.'

Kay sniffed, and Larch shoved a box of tissues across the desk towards her.

'Thanks.'

'We haven't always seen eye to eye, Hunter. But I respect Sharp, and he obviously respects you. So, what are you going to do to get him back?'

Kay blew her nose, scrunched up the tissue, and tossed it into the waste paper basket.

She took a deep breath, and forced herself to refocus.

'Right. Okay, well, I don't believe that Carl Ashton had anything to do with Jamie's death. He was reliant on Jamie for that extra income from the drugs they were bringing in. He confirms that he has no idea who Jamie was selling to, and after interviewing the adjutant, I don't believe he was involved either. The senior officer who probably helped Jamie smuggle the drugs into the country died some time ago, and again, from speaking with Ashton I don't think that man knew who the buyer was, either. With the restricted time we've had to investigate this, we haven't yet had a chance to speak to Jamie's friends – the non-army ones. Starting next week, we'll begin interviewing them. Hopefully that will shed some light.'

'Is there anything to suggest that Sharp covered this up?'

'It appears that Sharp tried to raise the matter with Harrison ten years ago, but was ignored. From talking with Sharp, it transpired that the investigation into Jamie's activities had only recently started when he was killed. Sharp had very little evidence to support the theory Jamie was responsible for the drugs found in the empty fuel tank. He believes that's why Harrison refused to consider the possibility that Jamie was murdered. There's nothing on the database about the drug dealing, and it was only brought to my attention once I'd spoken with Jamie's old commanding officer. Sharp then confirmed it.'

Larch nodded, and leaned back in his chair while he contemplated the ceiling.

'I'm not prepared to hand over the running of this station to a complete stranger. We need Sharp back here. You need to find that buyer, Hunter. That's the key.'

'Will do, guv.'

'Dismissed.'

TWENTY-EIGHT

Kay blinked back tears and tried to focus on the traffic in front of her.

She had turned down the radio upon starting the ignition, the cheery music at odds with her bleak mood.

Her arm ached, reminding her that she was still weak, and still needed time to heal. She knew she was pushing herself health-wise, but she couldn't give up now.

The shock of Larch's news reverberated in her thoughts, and she wondered when it would be made public to the rest of the personnel working at the station.

She realised that he hadn't told her whether Sharp was aware of the circumstances that were now dictating the urgency of the investigation. She suspected not – knowing Larch, he wouldn't want to get Sharp's hopes up, in case Kay failed.

She swallowed, bile rising at the thought of letting him down.

When she had raised the idea of pursuing the cold case, she could never have imagined that it would thrust her into the front line so quickly, or with such catastrophic consequences if she couldn't prove that Sharp was right, and that Jamie Ingram had been murdered.

A car horn honked, and she realised the traffic lights had turned green.

She pressed her foot to the accelerator, cursing as a bus chose the exact same moment to pull out in front of her from the supermarket car park, and banged the heel of her hand on the steering wheel in frustration.

The bus driver drove off oblivious to the minor accident he had nearly caused, and she checked her mirrors before pulling away once more.

Her thoughts returned to the conversation that she had had with Zoe Strathmore, the psychiatrist.

She would never admit to the nightmares, nor to her misgivings about her role, and she resented having to keep the appointment. She hadn't slept properly since, and her exhaustion was starting to have a telling effect on her body.

She sighed and realised that the ten-minute journey to her house was going to take twice as long – the pouring rain and poor visibility had slowed traffic to a standstill through the town centre. All she wanted to do was get home, and curl up on the sofa with Adam and a glass of wine. She didn't even know if she wanted to eat.

She choked out a laugh at the thought of Adam's face if she suggested such a thing – he was always teasing her about her eating habits, and would be mortified if she skipped dinner.

Her heart swelled at the thought of him, and she made a pact with herself that when the current investigation was over, she'd treat him to a weekend away.

They had had a week in Portugal in January; a cheap package deal that he had found online. She had protested at first, until he pointed out that a change of scenery would do her good once the plaster cast was removed from her broken arm.

They had resolved to take more holidays this coming year, and she felt her shoulders relaxing as she thought about the places they could explore.

She had a brief respite from the rain thundering on

the roof of the car as the traffic jam stopped and she found herself under the railway bridge across the A20.

A train rumbled across, sending pigeons flapping from their roost on the bridge rafters above her head.

She glared at them, daring them to crap on her car, but they settled without incident and the traffic moved forward.

Her mobile phone began to ring in its holder on the dashboard, and she recognised her sister's phone number. She flicked the switch on the steering wheel.

'Hey, Abby.'

'Oh my God, where are you? It sounds like you're standing under a waterfall or something.'

'I'm on my way home – it's pouring with rain, and the traffic is terrible. How're things with you?'

'Have you spoken to Mum today?'

Kay sat up straighter in her seat, alarm bells ringing in her head. 'She hasn't phoned me, no.'

The relationship between her and her mother hadn't improved over time. Once her mother had discovered the true effects of the aftermath of the Professional Standards investigation Kay herself had been subjected to two years ago, and the fact that Kay had miscarried and not told her parents at the time, her mother had refused to speak to her.

Abby sniffed. 'It's Dad.'

'What? What's going on? Is he okay?'

'They think so. He got rushed into hospital this morning with chest pains. I can't believe she didn't tell you.'

'Is he okay? Do you need me to be there?'

'No, it's okay – really. They're putting it down to a bad case of heartburn, but they're keeping him in overnight. Sorry if I frightened you.'

'Are you sure?'

'Yes. I just wanted to let you know in case you heard a rumour about him and panicked. You know what Aunt Liz can be like.'

Their dad's sister was a hypochondriac at the best of times, and if she had nothing to worry about with regard to her own health, her attention turned to her family. She could easily turn a case of bad indigestion into a quadruple bypass, given half the chance.

'Just as well you got hold of me before she did.'

'Yeah, look. I've got to go – the kids are about to start fighting. Dad will be home tomorrow night, if you want to give him a call then. I'll be popping round there, so I'll keep Mum busy when you phone.'

'That's great, Abby – thanks. Talk then.'

Kay finished the call, and realised her hands were shaking.

She indicated right off the main road, and followed the winding street through the housing estate before taking a left into the lane.

Adam's four-wheel-drive vehicle was parked on the gravel driveway, and she braked next to it before switching off the engine.

She sighed with relief. She loved her job, but there were some days when she was glad to be home.

When she pushed her key into the lock and stepped into the hallway, the first thing she noticed was the silence.

Downstairs was in darkness, save for a light on in the kitchen.

There were no aromas filling the house, no clang of pots and pans, nothing at all.

Frowning, she dropped her bag onto the stairs and hurried through to the kitchen.

Adam sat at the worktop, his head in his hands, a glass of untouched wine at his elbow.

He'd been crying.

'Adam? What on earth is the matter? What happened?'

He lifted his head, tears rolling down his cheeks.

'Rufus died this afternoon.'

Her bottom lip quavered, and then she crossed the room to him in three strides.

'He wasn't in any pain,' he said. 'He just slipped away. One minute he was snoring his head off while I was reading the paper, and then I realised the room had gone silent.' He wiped at his cheeks. 'I *always* make sure I'm there for them at the end, stroking their fur or holding a paw. I wasn't there for him.'

'Oh, Adam.'

His arms wrapped around her as she buried her head against his shoulder.

'This has been the worst day ever.'

TWENTY-NINE

A light frost covered Kay's car when she left the house on Saturday morning, and she didn't envy Adam having to conduct his weekly rounds of the local stable yards in the freezing weather after spending a late night liaising with the specialised pet crematorium service.

He'd left an hour before her, and once she'd pulled on a pair of jeans and a woollen jumper, she'd swept her handbag and keys from the kitchen worktop and headed out to work, her breath fogging on the cold air.

She was early; the upper level of the police station was in darkness when she arrived, and she spent five minutes switching on the coffee machine, her computer, and the printer and photocopier before removing her scarf. She kept her coat draped over her shoulders.

She cursed the electrical contractors who still hadn't fathomed the source of the problem with the central heating and air conditioning system, then wrapped her fingers around a mug of coffee and set to work.

She bit her lip as she scrolled through the new emails that had appeared on the system since she'd left the previous night, segregated the ones she could afford to ignore for a few days, and then began to delegate tasks to the team she now led while the ghost of Jamie Ingram plagued her thoughts.

Despite the result at charging the man who was working with him to supply drugs, she was still no closer to finding out the truth about his death, and it troubled her.

She was missing something; there was more to the case than they'd uncovered to date, and she cursed under her breath at her ineptitude at finding the link.

She hit "send" on the final email as Gavin pushed through the door, a takeout cup in his hand.

'Morning, Kay.' He placed a paper bag next to her elbow, the aroma of a warm croissant tickling her senses. 'Thought you might need that, given you don't eat breakfast.'

'Hey.' She raised her gaze to the grey light now filtering through the windows on the far side of the office, and blinked before checking her watch. 'Hang on. What are you doing in here on a Saturday? Are you getting behind on your workload or something?'

He grinned, opened his mouth to speak, and then turned as the door opened once more.

Carys and Barnes appeared, the younger detective blowing on her hands as she crossed the room.

'Flipping heck, it's supposed to be warming up at this time of year.'

Kay leaned back in her chair. 'All right, you lot. What's going on?'

'We reckoned you wouldn't be able to let things lie over the weekend,' said Barnes. He smiled. 'We know you too well.'

'Yeah, so we figured we'd come and help,' said Carys. 'Extra pairs of eyes and all that.'

Kay rubbed the back of her neck, some of the stress leaving her shoulders. 'I appreciate it, really I do. I'm not going to argue – I know none of you will listen anyway if I try to make you go home. But I'm treating you all to lunch up at the White Rabbit, okay? I'm not having you work this afternoon, otherwise you'll be exhausted when you come in on Monday.'

'Yes, guv,' said Gavin, and winked.

She screwed up the napkin next to her, and threw it at him, then turned serious and rose from her chair.

'Sharp's office.'

She waited until they had all settled, and then removed Carl Ashton's photograph from the whiteboard and set it to one side.

'All right, so after the events of yesterday, I'm satisfied that Ashton was not involved in the death of Jamie Ingram. Now we need to widen the investigation – that means re-interviewing his friends who Harrison's team spoke to at the time of his death. Who's got the names?'

Carys raised her hand, and lowered her gaze to a folder in her lap before flipping it open. 'Outside of the army, Jamie only had a couple of close friends – he had known Greg Kendrick since primary school, and apparently they used to catch the same bus to school. According to Natalie Ingram's original statement, Kendrick stayed in touch over the years, and visited the farm from time to time in between Jamie's deployments. A second person of interest, David Mason, lives in Canterbury and works at a large stationery warehouse. Married with two kids at the time of Jamie's death – apparently, he and Jamie were in the Scouts together as kids and, again, stayed in touch. Debbie has already spoken to them and obtained up-to-date details.'

'Good. In that case, I want you to spend the morning researching the background for these two. If you find anything – anything at all – then flag it so we can work it into our interviews with them next week.' She checked her watch. 'That gives us two and a half hours until lunchtime.'

'How did you get on with Larch yesterday?' said Barnes.

Kay took a sip of her coffee and contemplated her response before answering. 'Look, I'll be as honest as I can. There are going to be some big changes around here over the coming weeks. It's nothing to worry about – your roles are safe, but it does mean that we're under pressure to solve this case as soon as possible. We have to find the buyer, and we have to find out once and for all if that person was responsible for Jamie's death, or whether it was indeed a tragic accident.'

The team exchanged a glance between them, before Gavin turned back to her.

'Okay, what do you need from us?'

Kay smiled. 'Keep up the good work. We got a result yesterday – we're halfway there. I appreciate you're doing this in your own time, but we've got to keep going. We can't give up now, or allow ourselves to become distracted.'

Barnes raised himself from the visitor's chair, and stretched. 'All right, let's get on with it. What are you going to do in the meantime?'

'I'm going to speak to Michael and Bridget Ingram.'

THIRTY

Michael Ingram was standing at the door to the farmhouse as Kay braked to a standstill and climbed from her vehicle.

She peered over the roof, and noticed a pale blue car parked next to a small tractor, and recognised it from her visit to Natalie Stockton.

He held out his hand as she approached, his expression resigned.

'Thanks for seeing me at a weekend, I appreciate it.'

'Do you have any news? Have you arrested anyone?'

'Can we go inside? I see that Natalie's car is here.'

He nodded, and stepped back, closing the front

door behind her. 'She arrived about an hour ago with Giles and the kids.'

On cue, a child's excited screech reached her ears a moment before the sound of running feet from the room above.

Michael smiled. 'They're staying here for the weekend – Alex and Will are always a bit over the top when they first get here. They'll calm down in a bit.'

'It must be nice to have them all around you.'

'You're right, it is. Do you want to wander through to the kitchen? You know where it is – Bridget's in there. I'll nip upstairs and get Natalie. Giles can keep an eye on the children while we're talking.'

'Great, thanks.'

She waited until he had started to climb the stairs, and then made her way along the hallway and into the kitchen.

Bridget turned from the stove as she entered and pushed her hair out of her eyes.

'Morning, Detective. Michael said that you had phoned and would be calling in. Have a seat – make yourself comfortable. Cup of coffee?'

'That would be lovely, thank you.'

Kay shrugged her coat off her shoulders and hung

it over the back of a chair, and then took the steaming mug from Bridget and sat down.

A photograph album had been left open on the table, and Bridget wandered over when she noticed Kay casting her eyes over the pages.

'I haven't looked at these in an age,' she said, spinning the album around so Kay could see better. 'These were taken when the twins were teenagers.'

'They're younger here than in the photos Sharp has.'

'Yes – his were taken on their last day of secondary school. They were fourteen when these were taken.'

A sad smile passed the woman's lips as she turned the page. 'We had a record-breaking harvest that year, so it was all hands on deck. They used to get home from school at half past four, then help us in the orchards for a couple of hours before coming back inside to eat dinner and do their homework.'

She gently ran her hand over the page, and then glanced up as Michael appeared with Natalie.

The woman looked harassed, and took a seat opposite Kay with a loud sigh.

'Do you have children, Detective?'

'No, I don't. I take it they're excited to be here?'

'Yeah. Hopefully a few hours running around in

the farmyard with Dad later on will wear them out. It usually does – you can't beat fresh air.'

Kay waited until Michael and Bridget had joined them at the table, and then set down her mug and leaned forward.

'I wanted to speak to you today and provide you with an update with regard to how our investigation is progressing.'

'Have you arrested someone?' Michael repeated.

'We have, but not in relation to Jamie's death.' Kay gestured to Michael to stop him interrupting. 'Sorry, bear with me. After speaking with all of you, we began our investigation by re-interviewing Jamie's old army colleagues. I apologise – this is going to come as a shock to you, but during the course of our enquiries it transpired that Jamie was involved in smuggling drugs into the country after each deployment to Afghanistan.'

Bridget gasped, and covered her mouth.

'Drugs?' Natalie looked from her mother to her father, and then back at Kay, her eyes wide. 'Are you sure? Jamie would never do something like that. Where did you get that from?'

'The army had started its own investigation into the smuggling activities a short time before Jamie's death—'

'Sharp never said anything,' said Bridget. 'All this time. He never said anything.'

Michael reached out for his wife's hand. 'He spoke to me about it, after Jamie died. I didn't want to tell either of you because I was so scared what it might do to you – the shock.'

'Yesterday afternoon, we charged Jamie's co-conspirator, a man who has since left the army,' said Kay. 'I wanted to tell you face to face, before the media have had a chance to get their hands on the story. I will do my best to keep Jamie's name out of the papers, but I can't promise anything.'

'We know what the media can be like,' said Natalie, her top lip curling. 'We had a couple of them come around here after Jamie's death, wanting quotes and photographs. Dad sent them packing.'

'Where does that leave your investigation into Jamie's accident?' said Michael.

'My team are currently back at the station working through the other statements that were collated at the time from Jamie's friends. To date, we've been concentrating on the army connection, but it's now time to broaden our search.'

'Is there anything we can do?' said Bridget.

Kay tapped at the side of her coffee mug, and then met the woman's gaze. 'We've only got two names on file that were cited at the time as being close friends with Jamie. Greg Kendrick and David Mason. Is there anyone else that we should know about? It seems strange that he only kept in contact with two school friends after joining the army.'

'He was a shy boy,' said Bridget. 'I tried my best, really I did, but he preferred his own company. Despite being twins, he and Natalie were complete opposites.'

'I'm not aware of anyone,' said Michael. He shrugged. 'It's like Bridget says, Jamie was a quiet lad.'

'Hang on. Wasn't there a girl he was seeing at the pub close to the barracks?' said Natalie.

'What girl?' Bridget turned to her daughter. 'He never mentioned any girl to us.'

Kay pulled out her notebook, and flicked through the pages until she found her notes from her meeting with Jamie's ex-commanding officer. 'How well did he know her?'

'I know he mentioned buying her some diamond earrings, come to think of it.' Natalie slumped forward and held her head in her hands. 'My God – did he buy those with the money he was making from selling drugs?'

'I can't answer that for sure at this time,' said Kay. 'Do you have a name for her?'

Natalie raised her head. 'I can't remember. He only mentioned her the once, before he died. I know the name of the pub though – it was The Red Lion at Deepcut.'

'Thanks. I'll look into that.'

'What happens now?' said Michael.

Kay pushed back her seat, and drained her coffee. 'I'm heading back to the incident room now. We plan to speak with Jamie's friends early next week, and as soon as I have any further news for you, I'll be back in touch.'

Bridget followed her out to the front door, and stood on the step, hugging her thick woollen cardigan across her chest. 'My son was a good boy, Detective.'

Kay opened her mouth to respond, but the woman shook her head, and closed the door.

'Dammit.'

Kay stomped back to her car, cursing under her breath.

THIRTY-ONE

The following Monday, Kay elected to take Gavin
with her to interview David Mason, given that Carys
and Barnes had to spend the morning working on
their existing caseload rather than the decade-old
investigation she was leading.

Debbie had telephoned Mason the previous
afternoon, arranging for Kay to speak to him during
his lunch break.

On the way to Canterbury, Gavin had persuaded
Kay to stop at a petrol station so he could buy food.

She'd stared out of the window, watching other
drivers' vehicles as they tore past in the pouring rain
with no regard for their safety or that of others. At
one point, she'd had her heart in her mouth as a car
nearly aquaplaned across the asphalt.

When Gavin had returned to the vehicle, she had laughed as he tried to open the door and balance his purchases at the same time, cursing at the water that coursed down his neck.

As she pulled away, he had unwrapped the first of three sandwiches, devouring it with ease.

'Anyone would think you were starving.'

'I am. If I don't eat this, all you're going to hear during our interview with David Mason is my stomach rumbling.'

'I swear blind you've got hollow legs.'

He shrugged as he unwrapped the second sandwich. 'I've been working out a lot, ready for the summer. Me and some mates are saving up to go kite surfing down in Cape Town – if I don't keep my calories up, I won't be able to increase my strength.'

He polished off the last of the sandwiches, wiped his fingers on a paper napkin and shoved the rubbish in a plastic bag at his feet before extracting a printout that Debbie had handed to him on their way out the door.

Kay glanced over. 'So, what do we know about Mr Mason?'

Gavin raised his voice so she could hear him over the rain pounding the roof of the car. 'He's been working at the stationery superstore for the past four years – he's the manager there. Before that, he was a photocopier salesman travelling all over the Southeast. Lives in Canterbury, married with two kids – apparently the kids are now in their teens; a boy and a girl. The wife works at a biotech company as a personal assistant for one of the general managers.'

'All sounds normal, then.'

'Yeah – his name didn't come up in the database for anything, not even a traffic infringement.'

Kay slowed the vehicle as they approached the junction for the superstore, and silently congratulated herself as she found a parking space right outside the front door.

Gavin followed her through the glass double doors that opened automatically as they approached, and gave a low whistle under his breath.

'Debbie would call this paradise.'

Kay laughed, but had to agree with him – the uniformed police officer who helped them on many of their cases had a reputation for guarding the stationery cupboard as if it were the United States Bullion Depository at Fort Knox.

A salesgirl approached them, a smile on her face. 'Can I help you?'

'Morning,' said Kay. 'We've got an appointment to see David Mason at eleven o'clock.'

'Oh, right. He said he was expecting someone. Come with me – we've got an office at the back, and I think he said he was going to be there.'

Kay and Gavin followed the teenager through the length of the store, until she stopped at a solid wooden door, removed a lanyard from around her neck and swiped her security card across the lock.

A soft *click* reached Kay's ears, and the girl pushed the door open before gesturing to her right.

'Here you go. David's in there.'

'Thanks.'

David Mason rose from the chair he'd been occupying, and held out his hand as they entered. 'Thanks for being on time. I've got a telephone conference with head office in an hour.'

'That's fine,' said Kay. 'Hopefully this won't take too long.'

Mason moved across to the other side of the room, where a small coffee machine sat on a pine cabinet, and gestured to it.

'Hot drink?'

'That'd be great, thanks.'

Mason sorted out coffee for them, and then Gavin extracted his notebook as the superstore manager took a seat once more and pushed coffee mugs across the desk to them.

'The woman who phoned said you wanted to talk to me about Jamie Ingram.'

'Briefly, we've been requested to reopen the investigation into Jamie's motorbike accident ten years ago,' said Kay. 'I can't go into details, but I would like to know a bit about your relationship with Jamie – I understand that you'd known each other since you were at school?'

Mason tugged at his earlobe and leaned forward in his seat. 'Actually, we didn't hang out much at school. We were both in the Scouts. When we both left that at sixteen, we stayed in touch until Jamie joined the army.'

'Did you have much contact with Jamie once he joined up?'

'Not much. I saw him maybe once a year – usually around one of our birthdays. We got into the habit of meeting up for a quiet drink. It's strange; we really didn't have much in common, and I don't know if we would still be in touch if he was alive today.'

'When was the last time you spoke with Jamie?'

'The last time he came back from deployment. Thank goodness – after what happened, I'm glad that I got to see him that last time.'

Kay flipped through her own notes, and checked

the timeline. 'How many days before Jamie's death did you see him?'

'From memory, it was about six days. I didn't hear about the accident for a couple of days. I think it took Michael and Bridget time to get over the shock, before they started to contact Jamie's friends. Understandable, really.'

'Did Jamie seem concerned about anything when you saw him?'

His forehead creased. 'Yes, he did actually. We did our usual thing – met up for a couple of drinks at a pub here in Canterbury near the cathedral, and the whole time he kept checking his phone as if he was waiting for a phone call or text message. I remember that I joked that I needn't have bothered meeting him, given he wasn't really concentrating on the conversation. After that, he put the phone away, but he seemed nervous about it. When I asked him about it, he wouldn't tell me what was going on – I assumed it was something to do with the army. You know, perhaps they were getting ready to redeploy somewhere and he couldn't tell me where.'

'Have you stayed in touch with Jamie's family since?'

He shook his head. 'No – I wasn't really close to them. Like I said, I only knew Jamie because we'd both been in the Scouts together, and it did feel like we were drifting apart as friends when I last saw him.'

Kay rose to her feet, and signalled to Gavin.

'Thank you, Mr Mason. We won't keep you any longer.'

THIRTY-TWO

Kay and Carys had been shown to a meeting room upon arriving at the cement distribution depot north of Maidstone.

She'd left Gavin back at the incident room to type up his notes following their meeting with David Mason, and had smiled when he'd pulled out a large packet of muesli bars from his desk drawer as she'd left with Carys.

Greg Kendrick had explained to Carys when she had phoned him over the weekend that he worked as a delivery driver, often starting before six in the morning and then returning to the depot mid-afternoon.

The meeting room comprised a round table and four chairs, with a window that looked out onto the concrete apron of the distribution plant, a constant flow of cement trucks passing by.

The young girl that worked on reception had organised water for them, and as Kay drained the last dregs from her glass, the door to the room opened and a man stuck his head around it.

He wore a high visibility vest, glasses, and a harried expression.

He closed the door behind him. 'Sorry to keep you waiting – I'd hoped to finish early today because I knew you were waiting to speak to me, but we had an urgent last minute load to deliver in Aylesford. I'm Greg Kendrick.'

Kay shook hands with him, and introduced him to Carys before he took a seat opposite them and folded his hands on the desk.

'I understand you want to talk to me about Jamie Ingram?'

'Yes,' said Kay. 'I know you spoke to my colleagues about Jamie at the time of his death ten years ago, but as Carys told you on the phone, we've reopened the investigation into the motorbike accident, and I wanted to speak to his friends from that time.'

'Of course. What do you need to know?'

'Can you confirm how long you'd known Jamie for?'

'Since school. We both went to Swadelands in Lenham. Neither of us bothered staying on to do A Levels – Jamie joined the army soon after, and I've had a few labouring jobs over the years, before starting here four years ago.'

'Did you socialise much while he was in the army?'

'Yes, from time to time when he was on leave. You probably know this, but he spent a lot of his leave back at the farm – especially once he started being deployed to Afghanistan for months on end. I think he missed the greenery and the countryside. I knew his parents quite well from when we were at school, so I used to drive over to see him there, or would meet up and have a few beers in Maidstone.'

'May I ask, did you have a girlfriend or wife at the time? Did you socialise together with Jamie?'

'I was engaged at the time of Jamie's death. I hadn't seen him for a few months – he never met my wife.' He shrugged. 'Anyway, that didn't work out – we got divorced three years later.'

'Were you aware if Jamie was seeing anyone at the time?'

Kendrick leaned back in his chair and rubbed his chin. 'Yeah. I saw him nine days before he died, and that was the last time I saw him. He couldn't make it to Kent – said he had something on that meant he needed to stay close to the barracks for another couple of days – I don't know what. Anyway, I drove down to Surrey for the weekend and we went out for a drink. We went to the local pub – the Red Lion, I think it was called. There was a barmaid there who Jamie introduced me to, and it was pretty obvious that he was besotted with her. A few of us ended up having a lock-in on the Friday night, and they couldn't take their hands off each other. The landlord of the place let us crash out in his flat upstairs that night, and we had a big greasy fry-up in the morning. She hadn't stayed over – something to do with having to catch up with her family at some point that weekend, and she arrived later for her shift, but Jamie said over breakfast that he was going to ask her to marry him.'

Kay's heart skipped a beat. 'Did his parents know about that?'

Kendrick shook his head. 'I don't know. Jamie was still psyching himself up to ask her, so maybe he didn't tell them, in case she said "no".'

'Do you have a name?'

His brow puckered for a moment, and then his eyes lit up. 'Yes, I remember now – Amber Fitzroy.'

'Did he ask her while you were there that weekend?'

'No, that's the weird thing. On the Sunday afternoon as I was packing up my car to leave, I overheard loud voices in the kitchen. I had parked the car outside the back door of the pub, to keep the main car park clear for customers. Jamie and Amber were having one hell of an argument.'

'What about?'

'I don't know, but when I walked through the kitchen door, Amber ripped out some diamond earrings and threw them at him. She stormed out of the kitchen after that, and Jamie tried to laugh it off before ushering me back to my car. It was like he couldn't wait to get rid of me. I never did find out what it was all about.'

'Did you speak to her at all after Jamie died?'

'No. She didn't even turn up at his funeral, which I thought was strange.' He shrugged. 'I never went back to Deepcut after that – Jamie was the only person I knew that lived in the area, or at least at the barracks.'

'How would you describe his mood the last time

you saw him? Did he seem concerned about anything?'

'No. If anything, he seemed a bit full of himself – he was always pretty easy-going, but that last time he seemed to be going out of his way to show off. Most of the time he was happy to chat about the old days, and take the piss, but once he came into that money, he changed. It's like him giving Amber those earrings – he didn't have to do that. She'd said on that last Friday night while we were all drunk that she would have been happy with a meal out. Those earrings? Over the top, if you ask me.'

Kay exchanged a glance with Carys and then turned back to Kendrick. 'What do you mean "came into that money"? What money?'

'When I asked him how he could afford the earrings, he said that an aunt of his had died and left him with some money.' He shrugged. 'I guess he had a rich aunt. He'd never mentioned her before that, though.'

Kay closed her notebook, and signalled to Carys that they were finished. 'Well, thank you for your time. We won't keep you any longer.'

He rose from his seat, and then opened the door for them. As Kay drew level with him, he held up his hand.

'You didn't say why you had reopened the investigation into Jamie's motorbike accident.'

She gave a small smile. 'Routine, that's all. Thanks again.'

Kay waited until she and Carys had reached the car before she turned to the younger detective, who wore the same perplexed expression that Kay expected she had.

'So, Jamie lied to one of his oldest friends, using the same excuse Carl Ashton initially gave to you and Barnes to explain his sudden financial gain,' said Carys.

Kay opened the car door, tossed her bag into the foot well, and settled in for the ride back to the incident room.

'Makes you wonder what else he lied about – and why.'

THIRTY-THREE

Kay spun her chair from side to side as she waited for her call to be answered.

After four rings, and as she was about to give up, a gruff male voice barked a greeting.

'Mr Walsh?'

'Yes. That's me. Who is this?'

'Detective Inspector Hunter from Kent Police. Are you the current licensee for The Red Lion pub in Deepcut?'

'I am. What do you want?'

'We're currently in the process of reviewing a cold case from ten years ago. The motorcycle death of an army private who was based at the barracks that used to be there. I understand from talking to his ex-commanding officer and his sister that he used to drink in The Red Lion.'

The man snorted. 'He may have done, but that was before my time. I've only been here two years, and I'm about to put the place up for sale.'

'I don't suppose you know who ran the place ten years ago?'

'Yeah – that would have been Trent Oldham. He's retired now; the Lion was his last pub. He still lives in the village.'

'Have you got a number for him?'

'No. He's listed in the directory. You can look him up. If that's all, I have to go.'

He hung up without waiting for a response, and Kay glared at her phone in disbelief.

'I see your charm is working as well as ever,' said Barnes, grinning.

'Very funny. See if you can find a number for Trent Oldham.'

She waited while Barnes tapped his computer keyboard, his brow furrowed while he read the search results.

'How did you get on with Kendrick?' said Gavin, wandering over to her desk.

'Better than Mason – he's given us the name of

the barmaid who Jamie gave those diamond earrings to.'

'Here you go,' said Barnes. He handed Kay a sticky note with a phone number scrawled across it, and she wrinkled her nose.

'Christ, I can see why Debbie moans about your handwriting. What are you doing giving her your notes to type up, anyway?'

'She's faster than me.'

Kay waved the sticky note in his direction. 'Typing lessons for you, Detective Constable. As soon as possible. Notwithstanding the fact we have to get you kicking and screaming into the twenty-first century, Debbie's got better things to do than be your secretary.'

Gavin laughed, and wandered back to his desk as Barnes pouted at her.

She dialled the number on the note, and swore under her breath as it went to voicemail.

She knew she was becoming impatient, but she needed a result – and fast. She couldn't let Sharp or Larch down.

Not now.

She left a message, then slid her phone across the desk, resigned to having to wait for the ex-landlord to call her back, and instead began to sift through the paperwork in her trays.

'That's weird.'

Kay looked up from a prosecution report Gavin had prepared at Carys's voice, and noticed a perplexed expression on the DC's face.

'What is it?'

'When Harrison interviewed the Ingrams ten years ago, he never spoke to Giles Stockton. I can't find his name anywhere in the old database entries.'

'Natalie told us she didn't meet Giles until eight years ago.'

'Yeah, but he and Jamie knew each other.'

Kay pushed back her chair, the motion sending it scooting across the threadbare carpet until it hit a filing cabinet.

She ignored the noise, and hurried over to where Carys was staring at her computer screen.

'What have you got?'

'I was doing a routine search on Giles's background, and came across this photograph. It was taken at a fundraising event at the Hop Farm near Paddock Wood. Raised a lot of money for a local children's hospice – look.'

Kay peered over Carys's shoulder and stared at the photo on the screen.

In it, a smiling Giles Stockton had an arm slung around Jamie Ingram's shoulder, a huge grin on his face, and a glass of champagne in his hand.

Both men wore tuxedos, and looked comfortable in the formal attire – and in each other's company.

'Natalie never mentioned her husband knew Jamie at the time of his death,' said Kay, her interest piqued. 'When was this photo taken? '

Carys closed the photo file, returning to an archived news report. 'Here you go. Six months before Jamie died.'

'And six months before the drugs were found in the Jackal's fuel tank.'

Kay straightened, easing a crick in her back, and stared out of the window to the car park beyond.

The grey skies were beginning to darken, and a light drizzle was peppering the glass pane.

'What are you thinking, guv?'

'I'm thinking we need to speak to Giles Stockton.'

THIRTY-FOUR

Recalling that Natalie's husband commuted to the City on a daily basis, and keen to talk to Giles Stockton as soon as possible, Kay elected to drive to Yalding station and intercept him on his homeward journey.

At the back of her mind was Michael Ingram's warning that his daughter's grief had been detrimental to her health, and Kay didn't wish to interview Giles in front of Natalie so soon after their own conversation about her twin brother.

Carys had accompanied her, and was now staring out of the passenger window towards the entrance to the small country station.

As the day drew to a close, the temperature had

plummeted, so Kay left the engine running and the heater on.

West of the village and off the main road, the station served commuters travelling to London via Tonbridge. With only two platforms, it was easy for Kay and Carys to observe the arrival of the incoming trains, and they'd already found Stockton's top of the range vehicle parked under a street lamp within metres of the station's entrance.

All they had to do was wait.

Carys had phoned the bank that the economist worked at an hour and a half ago, on the pretext of wanting to arrange a meeting with him there.

The call had been short, and when she ended it, declining to leave a message with the receptionist, she had turned to Kay with a look of triumph.

'He left fifteen minutes ago. He's on his way.'

Now, the headlights of an approaching train lit up the track beyond their position and Kay reluctantly pulled the keys from the ignition and pushed open her door.

A bitter wind snapped at her coat as she buttoned it, and the two women hurried across the car park towards the ticket barrier.

'Makes you wonder why he doesn't drive to Tonbridge and take the train from there instead of having to change,' said Carys as she pressed her back against the brick structure of the station in attempt to escape the vicious breeze. 'It'd be quicker.'

'Have you seen the traffic through Hadlow and East Peckham these days?' said Kay. 'No – I reckon he's got the right idea.'

The train eased to a standstill a few metres from their position, and they stepped aside to let a small group of passengers exit through the gates.

Kay craned her neck, and saw the tall figure of Giles Stockton hurrying towards the barrier, his travel card ready.

An expression of surprise crossed his features when Kay approached him, her warrant card open.

'Detective Hunter? What are you doing here? Is everything all right with Natalie and the children?'

He swiped his card, then shoved it into his coat pocket and extracted a set of keys.

'Everything is all right with your family,' said Kay. 'I wondered if we might speak to you before you head home.'

'Ambush me, eh?' He consulted his watch. 'Well, I managed to catch an earlier train, so Nat won't be expecting me for another forty minutes. May I suggest we go to The George? I'm not well known there, so it'll be reasonably private, and it'll get us out of this godawful weather.'

'We'll follow you. Lead the way.'

Kay wasn't familiar with the pub Stockton had suggested, although she'd driven past it on a number of occasions.

In the light cast by the streetlights, she spotted the signage boasting riverside gardens, and made a mental note to perhaps explore it further with Adam when the summer began to venture once more into the countryside.

As she and Carys followed Stockton into the building, she admired the exposed stonework of the interior walls that were offset by a low painted ceiling and tiled floor.

A warmth emanated from the fire burning in a metal grate surrounded by a brickwork fireplace to her left, and at the sight of a menu displayed above the mantelpiece, Kay tried to ignore the hunger pangs that gnawed at her stomach.

Ten minutes later, Carys returned to the small table Kay had commandeered at the back of the pub, and passed Stockton half a pint of ale before placing two glasses of orange juice on the table and taking a seat next to Kay.

Kay thanked her, waited until she'd opened her notebook, and then turned her attention to Stockton.

'Natalie didn't mention that you knew Jamie Ingram before you were married to her.'

Stockton lowered his glass. 'Didn't she?'

Kay reached into her bag, and removed a copy of the photograph Carys had found before sliding it across the table to Stockton. 'Tell me about this. Did you know Jamie prior to this event?'

He took the picture from her before holding it up to the light. 'God, that was a night. I swear blind my hangover lasted for three days. In answer to your question, yes, but only in passing.'

'Did Natalie go to the fundraising event with you?'

'No – it was long before I met her and, anyway, she wouldn't have been allowed to go. It was for gentlemen only, see. Got a bit rowdy at one point, if you get my drift.'

'Not really, no. Elaborate, please.'

'Well, a couple of the chaps there played for the local rugby club. Organised a comedienne. Rather raucous, she was.' He blushed. 'I never told Natalie about it when I met her. She wouldn't have approved.'

'Did you keep in touch with Jamie Ingram after the event?'

'I can't recall, sorry. Of course, it's all so long ago now. One forgets.'

'Did you meet Natalie before or after her brother's death?'

'After. Poor girl was traumatised.'

'How did you meet her?'

He smiled. 'I bumped into her at a summer party at a mutual acquaintance's house on the other side of Wateringbury. Fabulous gardens. We were introduced by the hostess, and didn't stop talking with each other all night. It was rather lovely.'

'Did you tell her you knew her brother?'

'It must've slipped my mind.' He gave a small shrug, then raised his glass and drained a third of the ale.

'Have you ever taken drugs, Mr Stockton?'

'I beg your pardon?'

Kay remained silent, waiting.

He banged his glass on the table, and rose to his feet, glaring at her. 'How bloody dare you!'

'You didn't answer the question, Mr Stockton.'

He leaned over, swept his coat over his arm, and pointed a finger at her. 'Nor do I intend to. You're out of order. Next time you want to speak to me, Detective, it'll be in the presence of my solicitor.'

He snatched up his briefcase from the floor and spun on his heel.

Kay sipped her orange juice and watched as he tore open the door to the pub and stepped out into the night without a backward glance.

'What do you want me to do now, guv?' said Carys.

'Find out everything you can about Giles Stockton. Financial statements, employment records, the lot. Turn him inside out.'

THIRTY-FIVE

Kay stepped over the threshold to her home, closed the door behind her and leaned against it, exhausted.

Her mind was a jumble after speaking with Jamie's friends and Giles Stockton over the course of the day.

She had hoped the conversations would give her the breakthrough she so desperately needed. Instead, all she had done was learn that Jamie had indeed been afraid of someone – probably the buyer or buyers of the drugs he'd been supplying – but died before he'd had a chance to speak to anyone about it.

Now, she fully supported Sharp's theory that Jamie's death had been anything but an accident.

Someone had killed him to ensure his silence

about the drug operation that had proved to be so lucrative.

'Are you going to stand there all night?'

Adam peered around the kitchen door, a bottle of beer in his hand and a wide grin on his face.

'I'm too tired to move, so yes – I might.'

'You're going to have to get out the way at some point. Takeaway again, I'm afraid – I only got home myself twenty minutes ago, so it's Chinese tonight. The delivery bloke will be here in a while.'

Kay pushed herself away from the door. 'In that case, I'm going to get changed, and then I'm going to collapse.'

His laughter rang in her ears as she made her way upstairs.

While she changed out of her suit and into jeans and a battered old sweatshirt, she mulled over the interviews.

It seemed that as Jamie became further entrenched within the drug smuggling operation, he had let his friendships slip away, and she believed both David Mason and Greg Kendrick had no idea the man had been undertaking illegal activities.

Her thoughts returned to the conversation she and Carys had had with Giles Stockton.

The man had seemed genuinely outraged when

she had mentioned drugs, but she wondered why he had never spoken to his wife about knowing her brother prior to his death. It troubled her that although he admitted that Natalie had been devastated by Jamie's passing, he had never thought to tell her.

'Oi. You'd better not be working in that office of yours up there.'

She smiled as Adam's voice carried up the stairs, and padded out of the bedroom and across the landing.

'Believe it or not, I wasn't kidding about being too tired to do anything else tonight,' she said. When she reached the bottom of the stairs, she put her arm around him and steered him towards the kitchen. 'Gimme wine. Now.'

He gave her a gentle shove towards the barstools arranged around the kitchen worktop, then opened the refrigerator and pulled out a bottle of Sauvignon Blanc, pouring a generous measure into a glass for her.

'Do I dare ask how your day went?'

She took a large sip before setting her glass down on the worktop, then reached into the pocket of her jeans, pulled out an elastic band that she always kept to hand, and tied her hair into a ponytail.

'Frustrating. I've spoken with three people today

– two of whom tried to be helpful, but couldn't shed any light on why an old friend of theirs was behaving out of character before his death, and the other has raised more questions that could send this investigation off down yet another path. And, if I'm right about him, things could get ugly.'

Adam's brow furrowed, and she decided to change the subject – there was no sense in worrying him about the state of her investigation.

'What about you? What have you been up to?'

His face grew serious. 'I spoke to Rufus's foster carers today. They got back from Wales last night, so you can imagine how that went.'

Kay reached across the worktop and wrapped her fingers around his.

He squeezed her hand. 'Anyway, apart from that it was a quiet day – I managed to get some time to myself and work on that journal article I've been trying to write for the past three weeks. The deadline is in two days' time, but hopefully I'll gain some exposure for the practice from it when it's published.'

He ran a hand through his black curly hair, his dark eyes gleaming. 'And, in better news, I met with the accountant this afternoon, and we're showing a twenty per cent increase on last year's takings for the business.'

Kay held up her glass and clinked it against his bottle of beer. 'That's brilliant. You've worked so hard for it, well done.'

'Thanks. I was surprised actually, given that we've taken on an extra vet. Mind you, the overheads are down, and it all seems to be ticking along nicely.'

He stretched, his long-sleeved T-shirt riding up across his stomach, and then yawned before he turned away from the worktop and slid the empty beer bottle into the recycling bin before helping himself to a glass of wine and wandering back to her.

His hand moved to the back of his neck as he closed his eyes for a moment, and Kay felt an enormous sense of pride in the man she shared her life with.

The past two years hadn't been easy for either of them, and yet they'd stuck together, never giving up, and determined to succeed.

Adam opened his eyes at the sound of the doorbell; at the same time Kay's stomach rumbled.

His mouth quirked. 'I'm not even going to ask if you remembered to eat today. The sooner Sharp is back, the better – the others are useless at nagging you.'

Kay aimed a mock punch his way, but he shifted too fast and wandered out to the hallway, laughing.

She could hear his voice at the door, talking to the man that delivered their food while she fetched cutlery and plates from the cupboards, setting them out on the worktop as Adam reappeared.

They ate in silence for a while, sharing out the food from the containers and enjoying each other's company.

Eventually, Adam pushed his empty plate away, and sighed. 'I needed that. So, what will you do next with your investigation?'

Kay put down her knife and fork, and rested her chin in her hand.

'There's nothing else for it. We're going to have to go through everything we've done so far and review it. Someone, somewhere, isn't telling us the truth. Starting with Natalie Stockton's husband.'

THIRTY-SIX

'Inspector?'

Kay didn't register the voice at first, still unaccustomed to her new rank and instead remained intent on her work until Barnes coughed and waved his hand in her direction.

'He's talking to you, Hunter.'

Kay tore her eyes away from her computer screen to see Sergeant Hughes standing at the door to the incident room, a hopeful expression on his face.

'What's up?'

'There's a woman at the reception desk who says you wanted to talk to her about Jamie Ingram?'

'Amber Fitzroy?' said Barnes.

'That's her,' said Hughes. 'I said you'd be right down, if that's okay?'

'Absolutely fine. Is there an interview room free?' She picked up her mobile phone and notebook, and then threaded her way between the desks, tapping Barnes on the shoulder as she passed him.

'You can use number four,' said Hughes, and grinned. 'Good job it's quiet this week. The cold weather keeps most of the idiots at home this time of year.'

She could still hear him chuckling to himself as she reached the corridor and hurried down the stairs, closely followed by Barnes.

She paused on the bottom step and turned to him.

'Trent Oldham must've passed our message on. I expected to speak to her on the phone first and drive up to Surrey.'

'I've got to admit, she's keen if she's turned up here in person out of the blue. What do you think?'

'I want you to lead this one. Be nice. It might just be the case that she and Jamie were close, but let's find out if she knew anything about the drug smuggling.'

Barnes straightened his tie and buttoned his jacket. 'Okay. Let's go.'

When Kay pushed open the door into the reception area of the police station, Amber Fitzroy was pacing the floor in front of the desk rather than waiting in one of the plastic chairs.

She turned at the sound of voices, and Kay was struck by the anxious expression on the woman's face.

After introducing herself and Barnes, she ushered Amber towards the interview rooms and waited while she settled into a chair, opening her notebook.

Barnes gave Amber a brief overview of their investigation, and thanked her for coming in to see them.

'We'd like to have a chat with you about the time you were working at the Red Lion Inn at Deepcut,' he said. 'When did you start working for Trent Oldham?'

Her mouth quirked. 'When I was sixteen and a half. I was tall, and he always paid in cash, so it didn't matter to him that I was under age. I never drank in the pub anyway, not until my eighteenth birthday.'

'Do you still work there?'

'No. I left the Deepcut area six months after Jamie's death. The gossip in the village surrounding Jamie became too much, and I moved away to the other end of the county. I met my husband, Mark, at a local gym and we got married four years ago. We've got a couple of kids now – a boy, who's four and an older girl, who's seven.'

'You kept your surname?'

'Yes. I like it, and Mark didn't mind. He's quite laid-back about things like that.'

'We understand that you and Jamie Ingram were close. How long had you known him for?'

The woman tucked a strand of dark brown hair behind her ear, and then hugged her arms over her white woollen coat that she had declined to remove.

Kay couldn't blame her – the interview rooms were freezing cold, and she rued the fact she hadn't worn a warmer jacket that day.

'About eighteen months,' said Amber. A sad smile crossed her features. 'I'd been working there about three years when Jamie first turned up. 'He wasn't like the others. You could tell he had a good upbringing. Some of the soldiers who used to drink in the pub were a bit rough around the edges.'

'How long were you his girlfriend for?'

'We got together about three months after he first started drinking there. Like I said, he was different to a lot of them. He used to like sitting by himself in the corner, just daydreaming sometimes. I got chatting to him one night, and it went from there. I hated it when he went overseas – I know his job didn't put him in direct danger, but he was still out there. I can't begin to describe the relief I felt every time he walked through the door on his return.'

'How serious would you say your relationship was with Jamie?'

She sighed, and uncrossed her arms. 'You heard about the diamond earrings?'

'We did.'

'He gave them to me for my birthday. I couldn't believe it – it was obvious they weren't a cheap knockoff. I was embarrassed, to be honest. His birthday had been four months before that, and all I could afford to get him were some books and a nice cashmere scarf I'd seen online.' She pulled a paper tissue from the pocket of her coat and blew her nose. 'Anyway, once I got over the shock, I quite liked the idea of being spoilt like that. I was working that night – it was a Friday – and it was fun flashing them under the noses of some of the women. You should've seen their faces.'

'When did it go wrong? We heard that you and Jamie had an argument sometime after he gave you the earrings.'

Her bottom lip trembled. 'It was a while after he gave them to me. He was already back in Afghanistan. I don't know why, but I thought I'd better get them valued. I've never owned anything like it, and my mum mentioned to me that we ought to look at getting them put on the home and contents insurance. I've never been so shocked in my life. They were worth a fortune. Of course, then I started worrying about how he'd afforded them in the first place. I knew he didn't earn much in the Royal Logistics Corps, so it didn't make sense.'

As tears welled in the woman's eyes, Kay pushed a fresh box of tissues across the table to her.

Amber nodded her thanks, composed herself, and then continued.

'I confronted him in the pub one morning after he'd returned to England. I didn't think anybody had heard us – I waited until his friend had gone out to his car. I'd been psyching myself up to speak to him, and he was on his way back to the barracks, so I was almost out of time. He told me that I shouldn't worry about it, but there was plenty more money where that came from. He said that people depended on him. He said that he wanted to make a life for us together, and that wasn't going to happen on army pay.'

She dabbed at her eyes. 'Of course, by then everyone had heard the rumour about the drugs bust at the barracks. I put two and two together, and realised he'd probably been involved, so I asked him. He didn't deny it – he almost seemed proud of the fact that he had outsmarted everyone. I was livid. I threw the earrings back at him and told him he had to stop, that he had to tell his commanding officer what he knew about the smuggling operation, but I think by then it was too late. He seemed terrified. I'll never forget it. He said, "I can't back out. They'll kill me".'

THIRTY-SEVEN

Several hours later, Kay held her head in her hands and shivered as the cassette tape whirred in the machine.

There was nothing wrong with the heating now – the contractors had finally fixed the fault, and the room temperature was returning to normal. Instead, it was the voice emanating from the loudspeakers that sent a chill down her spine.

DCI Simon Harrison had been a detective constable at the time of Jamie Ingram's death, and as she progressed through the recording of him interviewing Glenn Boyd the day after the motorcycle accident, bile rose in her throat while she listened to the man who used her to trap Jozef Demiri, and nearly got her killed in the process.

She could hear the sneer in his voice as he questioned Boyd about Jamie's riding skills and put it to him that he had been speeding without due care and attention for the road conditions.

Boyd seemed to accept Harrison's suggestion, and Kay cursed under her breath at the detective's poor witness interview techniques.

Earlier, Amber Fitzroy had waited in the relative warmth of the reception area while her statement had been typed up, and Kay had asked her if she had plans to stay in the area for a couple of days, in case the investigating team had further queries.

Amber had agreed willingly to Kay contacting her again if she needed to. 'I'd made arrangements with Mark for him to get his mum to look after the kids before I left because he couldn't get time off work. I'm staying at the Hilton in Bearsted for a couple of nights – I thought I might see if I could call in to see Michael and Bridget while I'm here.' She dropped her gaze. 'I can't believe it's been ten years. I really should have contacted them before now. The problem was, I never really knew what to say to them after Jamie died. He never got the chance to introduce me to them when he was alive, and I was too embarrassed by that to go to Jamie's funeral. I want to apologise to them.'

A thought had struck Kay at the woman's words. 'One of Jamie's friends mentioned that he was planning on asking you to marry him.'

A sad smile had crossed Amber's lips. 'It's true. He told me as much that last time we argued.'

'Did his family know?'

'I don't think so, no.'

After making sure Amber signed her statement, and swapping mobile phone numbers with her, Kay had excused herself and returned to the incident room, collecting copies of the tapes from Harrison's previous investigation and returning to the interview room in the hope of listening to them without being disturbed.

She sighed, and threw her pen onto the table as the interview with Glenn Boyd finished. Ejecting the tape, she returned it to its plastic case, and lined it up alongside the others.

After two hours, she was none the wiser about Jamie's drug dealing business, his buyer, or his killer.

She rocked back on her chair and rubbed the back of her neck. She knew she should rest; her thoughts were going around in circles, and she needed to take a break. Checking her watch, she was surprised to see that it was already six o'clock.

Gathering up the paperwork and the box of tapes,

she made her way back to the incident room and dumped the cassettes on Debbie's desk.

'Any luck?' said the police officer, sliding the box out of her way.

Kay shook her head. 'I thought I might have missed something the first time around. I was wrong.'

'Ah, well. Worth checking, I suppose.'

'Guv?'

Kay glanced over her shoulder, to see Carys waving her over.

She held up a manila folder as Kay approached. 'I finished those searches about Giles Stockton.'

'Please, tell me you found something.'

'I hit the jackpot,' said Carys, a broad grin on her face.

Kay sank into a spare chair as she took the folder. 'What do you mean?'

'A little under eleven years ago, Stockton was pulled over at a routine traffic stop on the A26 west of Wateringbury.'

'Drink driving?'

'No – but the attending officer reported Stockton was in an agitated state, and being evasive when questioned. They searched the car, and found some cannabis in the glove compartment.'

Kay's heart skipped a beat. 'How much?'

'Enough for personal use only, but he was expected to appear before a magistrate six weeks later.'

'"Expected to"? What happened?'

Carys leaned over and tapped her finger on the final paragraph of the pages she'd printed out. 'The charges were dropped two weeks before he was due in court.'

'What? How?'

'Someone intervened and requested that the matter be reviewed. A new detective was tasked with the job, and the charges were then dropped.'

Kay's eyes narrowed. 'Who was the investigating officer?'

'Simon Harrison.'

THIRTY-EIGHT

'How the hell do those two know each other?' said Kay.

'I was thinking about that, and then I wondered if perhaps it's something to do with that event at the Hop Farm,' said Carys. 'The one we know Stockton attended with Jamie Ingram.'

'Do you think that's the first time they met, or did they know each other beforehand?'

Carys shrugged. 'There's nothing else in the system.'

'All right,' said Kay. 'Get onto the Hop Farm. Request a copy of all attendees that were there that night. The place has been doing events like this for years, so I'm hoping they keep all the records on their system for marketing purposes.'

'Will do.'

Kay rose from her seat and checked her watch. 'Great work, by the way. Call them in the morning – there'll be no-one there now who can help you, and I want you back here early to follow up your theory. Let me know as soon as you have anything.'

'Thanks, Kay. No problem.'

Kay wandered back to her desk and texted Adam.

She had one more thing to do before heading home, and she was determined to make some headway in the investigation.

————

Rebecca Sharp opened the door moments after Kay rang the doorbell, and smiled when she saw the detective.

'Hi, Kay. Is Devon expecting you?'

Kay wiped her feet on the mat and waited while Rebecca closed the door. 'No – sorry, I didn't mean to disturb you both. I wondered if I could have a quick word with him.'

'I won't be dishing up dinner for another forty minutes. Come on through – he's in the office.'

Kay followed Rebecca through the house and into

the couple's dining room, which Sharp had transformed into an office for himself.

He rose from his chair, his hand outstretched. 'Everything okay?'

'I wondered if I could have a word?'

Rebecca smiled, and turned on her heel. 'I'll leave you two to it.'

'Sorry, Bec. I won't keep him long,' said Kay.

Sharp waited until the door closed behind her, then gestured to Kay to take the spare chair under the window.

'Thanks.'

'What's going on?'

Kay took a deep breath before continuing. 'Did you know that Jamie Ingram and Giles Stockton knew each other?'

His brow furrowed. 'No, I didn't. How did you find out?'

'Carys found a photograph taken of the two of them at an event at the Hop Farm. Some sort of charity event. Do you know if Jamie introduced Giles to Natalie before he died?'

'No. As far as I was aware, Natalie met Giles a couple of years after Jamie's death at a friend's party in Wateringbury.'

'You're absolutely sure?'

'Yes. She was over the moon about him when they met – she insisted on introducing him to me and Rebecca at the same time as her parents. We were having lunch together at the farm, and she brought him over as a guest.' He leaned forward and rested his elbows on his knees. 'Why?'

She shook her head. 'I'm not sure at the moment. We're still looking into it, and I don't understand it all yet. Were you aware that Simon Harrison had got Giles Stockton off charges of cannabis possession a few months before Jamie's death?'

Sharp's mouth thinned. 'I wasn't with the police then, as you know. And, no – I didn't.'

Kay rose from her chair, unable to sit still. Leaning against the door, she cast her eyes over the commendations and photographs from Sharp's military career and subsequent rise through the Kent Police ranks.

'The thing is, Devon, I have three people who are all connected – Jamie, Giles Stockton, and Simon Harrison. I have a supplier – Jamie, with his army colleague Carl Ashton; I have a potential buyer in Giles, and I have a crooked detective who might have covered for them. What I don't have is a motive for Stockton or Harrison to kill Jamie. What could they possibly have gained by doing that?'

Sharp straightened, and he cleared his throat. 'Maybe you need to look at this a different way. Maybe it's not about who had the most to gain, but who had the most to lose if Jamie was out of the way.'

Kay pushed away from the door and picked up her bag. 'Thanks, guv. I think it's time we formally interviewed Giles Stockton.'

THIRTY-NINE

Kay pushed through the door to the incident room the next morning with a renewed focus.

She placed her take-out coffee cup next to her desk phone and switched on her computer before removing her coat and hanging it over the back of her chair.

The rest of the team began to filter in as the clock on the wall drew closer to eight o'clock, and an hour later, the room was filled with the buzz of activity as different investigations were progressed.

Carys leapt from behind her desk moments after her computer *beeped* with the sound of an arriving email and headed towards Kay, her excitement palpable.

'The Hop Farm sent over the guest list for that

event Jamie Ingram went to,' she said, handing Kay a printout. 'Simon Harrison is on there as well.'

Kay scanned the list until she saw his name. 'That's brilliant, well done.'

She handed back the printout, and called across the room to Debbie.

'Did you manage to get hold of Giles Stockton?'

'He's booked in for interview in about twenty minutes,' the uniformed officer said. 'He's bringing his solicitor with him.'

'Thanks, Debbie.'

'How do you want to approach this?' said Carys.

'With care. He's already confirmed to us that he met Jamie at that event, so we need to get that on the record. I want to find out how they first met, and why those charges were dropped against him. Then, I need to find out what the connection is between him and Simon Harrison.'

The phone on her desk began to ring, and she leaned across to answer it.

'We'll be right down.' She replaced the receiver, and turned to Carys. 'Stockton and his solicitor are here. I'll lead, but give me a signal if there's something you want to ask him.'

They made their way down to the reception area, signed in Stockton and introduced themselves to his solicitor, a man who Kay hadn't met before, but immediately took a dislike to after shaking hands with him and having her fingers crushed.

She glared at the back of his head as Carys led them through to the interview room, and then waited while they took their seats.

Carys switched on the recording equipment before Kay read out the formal caution.

Kay pushed across the photograph of Stockton with Jamie Ingram at the Hop Farm. 'Please confirm for the record that this picture shows you with Jamie Ingram.'

'That's correct.'

'When was this taken?'

'About six months before he died, at a private fundraising event.'

'How did you meet Jamie Ingram?'

'At a Chamber of Commerce meeting. We were approached by the woman organising this fundraiser, and agreed to attend. Jamie's father wasn't interested – not his thing, he said. My father was still alive back then, and donated one of the raffle prizes. A day out at the races, if I recall correctly. All good fun.'

'You say that Jamie's father wasn't interested in attending. Did you know Michael Ingram at that time?'

'No – I was simply paraphrasing what Jamie told me at the time.'

'What did you and Jamie discuss at the event?'

He snorted. 'Honestly, Detective, I can't remember. It was years ago. Can you remember what *you* talked about ten or eleven years ago?'

She ignored the question. 'Did you socialise with Jamie a lot?'

'No, I didn't. I didn't even know this photograph existed until you showed it to me.'

'Do you try to avoid being photographed, Mr Stockton?'

The solicitor cleared his throat. 'I fail to see what that question has to do with your current enquiries.'

Kay kept her gaze levelled at Stockton, refusing to react to the solicitor's protests. Instead, she opened the folder she had brought with her, and slid Stockton's original charge sheet across the table to him. She tapped the page.

'You were arrested for possession of cannabis before Jamie died.'

Stockton flung his hands up in the air. 'This is outrageous. Those charges were dropped before it even got to court.'

'Yes, and I'd like to understand the reason why.'

'I don't know – you'll have to ask Harrison.'

Kay smiled as Stockton's face paled when he realised his mistake. She took the charge sheet from him, and returned it to the folder before closing the flap and resting her hands on it.

'How long have you known Simon Harrison?'

'I don't know what you mean.' Stockton's fingers played with the knot of his tie, the colour returning to his face.

'Two weeks before you were due to appear at Maidstone magistrates' court facing charges of cannabis possession, Simon Harrison conducted a case review that resulted in those charges being dropped against you. How much did you pay him?'

The solicitor slammed his hand on the table and leaned forward. 'You had better have evidence to support that accusation, Detective.'

'It's okay, Andrew.' Stockton turned his focus back to Kay. 'I didn't pay anyone, and I have no idea why the charges were dropped. What I do know is that I am truly grateful that I got a second chance. I made a stupid mistake and it nearly cost me my career.'

'Are you in the habit of taking drugs on a regular basis, Mr Stockton?'

The solicitor rose from his seat and placed a hand on his client's shoulder. 'Don't answer that.' He turned to Kay, a sneer on his face. 'Detective, are you going to charge my client with something?'

Kay shook her head, but kept her gaze levelled at Stockton. 'No. We're done. For now.'

———

'How did it go, Kay?'

Barnes joined her at the window of Sharp's office and jerked his chin at the retreating figures of Giles Stockton and his solicitor as they walked to their cars.

'We've got him, Ian. He's on the record now acknowledging he knew Jamie Ingram for about six months before he died. Then he slipped up, and confirmed before I asked him that Simon Harrison arranged to drop the cannabis possession charges against him.'

'Where does that leave us?'

She bit her lip while the solicitor shook hands with Stockton before he climbed into his vehicle and drove out of the police station car park.

Stockton remained standing next to his vehicle, his hands in his pockets as he glared at the back door to the building.

'Right now, I reckon he's panicking. He can't speak with Harrison – he's being held in custody in an open prison for the next four months while the investigation into the shooting of Jozef Demiri is concluded.'

'I'll make a call to the prison anyway, and request that they let us know if Harrison receives any visitor requests.'

'Good idea.' She turned away from the window as Stockton finally opened his car door and got in. 'We need evidence that he was the buyer, Ian. It's too circumstantial at the moment – I'll never get Jude to take it on if we don't come up with something to prove this case.'

FORTY

Kay suppressed a yawn and turned the page of a report she was meant to have read three days ago, and only because the author of it had phoned her an hour ago seeking her feedback.

She wouldn't have minded, except that the subject matter was drier than the Gobi Desert, and it was keeping her from reviewing her team's caseload.

She skimmed over the final page and tossed it into the top tray on her desk with a groan, and then printed out the comments sheet she was meant to return before the end of the day. Once she'd scribbled a note of her thoughts across the page, she opened her desk drawer, reached inside, and cursed aloud.

'You all right?' said Debbie as she wandered past.

'Bloody Barnes has nicked my stapler again.'

Carys laughed, and wandered over with her own stapler. 'Here, use this.'

'Thanks. I swear blind I'm going to put a lock on this drawer. For a copper, he's got incredibly sticky fingers. Did you sort out those typing lessons for him, Debs?'

The uniformed officer grinned. 'I haven't told him yet. He's got three days' solid training next week.'

'Good. That's what I call karma.'

Kay handed back the stapler, and then peered into her desk drawer to find a black pen with which to sign off the report. Her brow furrowed at the sight of a business card that lay face down under a hole punch, and she reached out for it before turning it in her hand.

'Jonathan Aspley. I'd forgotten about you.'

She cast her mind back to the beginning of the winter when she and the team had been in the final throes of their investigation into Jozef Demiri. She had been approached by a local reporter who had told her about Simon Harrison's reputation for putting his own officers in danger.

Her mistake had been not to pay heed to his warning.

She glanced up, but Carys and Debbie were deep

in conversation, so she pulled out her mobile phone and dialled the number on the card.

Aspley answered immediately. 'Detective Hunter – I was glad to hear you were back at work. How are you?'

'Hungry, and I need food. Interested?'

'Where?'

'Out of town. Where we won't be overheard. Do you know The Tickled Trout at West Farleigh?'

'Yes.'

'Last one there buys lunch.'

She ended the call, pulled her jacket off the back of her chair, and swung her bag over her shoulder.

'If anyone is after me, I'll be back in a couple of hours,' she said to Debbie as she passed her desk, and hurried out to her car.

She relished the drive to the countryside pub, a firm favourite of hers.

As she turned off the Tonbridge Road at Teston and drove over the railway crossing, she glanced out of her window at the river that bisected the water meadows.

A narrowboat meandered along the water course, and she wondered what the occupant did for a living that meant he could spend his time relaxing in such a way.

She slowed as she approached the narrow stone bridge that crossed the Medway, pleased to note a van travelling from the opposite direction paused to let her pass with a flash of its headlights. She held up her hand in thanks to the driver, and accelerated up the lane.

Within moments, the painted white façade of the pub came into view, its brick chimneys soaring above a russet-coloured tiled roof.

She pulled into the car park behind the pub, and noted with satisfaction that she had beaten the journalist.

His car appeared as she was locking her door, and he hurried over to join her, a smile on his face.

'I hope you weren't speeding, Detective.'

'No need to be a bad loser, Aspley.'

He grinned and held open the door to the pub for her.

Kay unbuttoned her jacket as the warmth of the pub began to ease the cold from her body, and stood at the bar with the journalist while they ordered their food.

He handed her drink to her, and gestured to a table next to the window. 'Shall we?'

'Thanks.'

'When did you get back to work?'

Kay dumped her bag and jacket on the plush seat next to hers, and rested her elbows on the table. 'A couple of weeks ago.'

'Settling back into it okay?'

'I guess so, yes.'

'I heard about Sharp. That was a rough deal, sorry.'

She shrugged. 'What have you been up to?'

'This and that. I'm working on a new story at the moment about illegally low wages in the fast food industry. Students and foreign workers are too scared to speak up for fear of losing their jobs most of the time, so it's hard to get anyone to talk to me about it.'

'Your career's going from strength to strength since I last saw you.'

'Yeah, well I think I got the better end of the deal. I got an exclusive story that went nationwide and accelerated my career, and you ended up nearly drowning. You were bloody lucky, you know that, right?'

'I do. Congratulations on the story, too. You did a good job.'

'Hey, thanks. That means a lot coming from you.' He broke off as the waitress brought their food over and they began to eat. 'Well, I'm guessing you didn't ask me to meet you to make small talk. What did you want to see me about?'

'Simon Harrison.'

'What about him?'

'Did any of your investigations into his past conduct uncover any evidence of substance abuse? Alcohol, drugs, or something?'

'What makes you say that?'

'I can't tell you at the moment, sorry.'

'What? I buy you lunch—'

'You lost a race—'

'If I'd known you had ulterior motives…'

'Oh, come on, Jonathan. Stop messing around. What else have you got on Harrison?'

He put down his knife and fork and picked up his glass instead, taking a sip of ale.

Kay resisted the urge to kick him under the table, and instead held her breath and waited.

'All right,' said Aspley. He checked over his shoulder, and when he saw the landlady had moved across to the other side of the bar, he turned back to Kay. 'A few years ago, a detective on Harrison's team suggested that the DCI might have a drug problem.'

'A habit, you mean?'

'Yeah. No evidence, though and no-one would talk to me about it. The bloke who first brought it to my attention was transferred out a couple of months later.'

'Frightened off?'

'Punishment, I think. Ended up in Reading.'

Kay pushed the last of her jacket potato to one side, picked up her orange juice and took a sip. 'A cocaine addiction might go some way to explain his gung-ho attitude towards his investigations.'

'What are you up to, Hunter? I heard you were meant to be on light duties at the moment.'

She smiled. 'You're the journalist. You know you shouldn't believe everything you hear.'

———

Kay swung her chair from side to side and tried to concentrate on the emails she was scrolling through.

She hadn't stopped rushing around the station to attend different meetings since returning from lunch, and although she'd never admit it to her colleagues, fatigue was starting to set in and take its toll.

She had waited until no-one was looking before reaching into her bag and removing two painkillers from the small bottle she'd been prescribed, swallowing the bitter pills with a mouthful of coffee.

Her arm ached, and she welcomed the sight of the clock's hands swinging round to six.

Ever since she'd left the pub at lunchtime, she'd been wondering about Aspley's information that Harrison was rumoured to have had a liking for recreational drugs.

Did Jamie Ingram have a falling out with Giles Stockton?

Had Stockton killed Jamie, before Harrison had helped him to cover up the crime? But, why?

Had Stockton been supplying Harrison's drugs? Had he threatened to blackmail him?

Carys began to clear her desk as Kay rubbed at her temples, the *clink* of crockery reaching her as the team began to tidy away for the night, carrying dirty dishes and tea mugs into the small kitchenette.

Kay sank into her chair, reached out and wiggled the mouse to wake up the computer screen, and then began to scan through the emails that had appeared in her absence.

Her phone vibrated on the desk, and she smiled as she read the text message from Adam.

Cooking a Thai curry. Ready in an hour X.

She looked up as Gavin burst through the door to the incident room and strode towards her desk, waving a page in the air.

'What's got your knickers in a twist?'

'Natalie Ingram. She hasn't been telling us the truth about her counselling sessions ten years ago.'

She pushed back her chair and gave a low whistle in the direction of where Barnes and Carys stood next to the kettle.

'Get yourselves over here.'

FORTY-ONE

Kay waited until the small team had filed into Sharp's office, then closed the door and gestured to Gavin.

'All right, Piper. Explain.'

'Okay, so I had some spare time this afternoon, and I thought I'd go through the statements we've had to date. This time around, I mean. Not the original documentation.'

'As a wise man once remarked, "get on with it",' said Barnes.

'Right, well. When you and Kay first spoke with Michael and Bridget Ingram to tell them we were reopening the investigation into Jamie's motorbike accident, Bridget told Kay that Natalie received three months' worth of counselling afterwards to deal with her grief. Natalie confirmed it when you caught up with her.'

Carys edged forward on her seat. 'Hurry up, Gavin.'

'Sorry. Anyway, I did a bit of digging around in the system, because none of them mentioned to us which counsellor she'd gone to. Lucky for us, one of the uniformed officers working on the original case with Harrison was smart – he found out that Natalie didn't go to a local counsellor. She opted to check in to a private clinic near Guildford for three months.'

'Guildford?' said Kay. 'Why on earth would she go all that way?'

'And why for so long?' said Carys. 'Surely she'd only have a couple of sessions a week or something like that? Why stay for three months?'

Gavin held up the document in his hand, a triumphant gleam in his eyes. 'Because she wasn't suffering from grief. I think she had a cocaine addiction.'

The shocked silence that followed was eventually broken by the sound of Barnes hissing through his teeth.

'Bloody hell.'

Kay took the page from him and scanned her eyes over his notes. 'Are you absolutely sure about this?'

'Yeah. I phoned the place. They've never offered grief counselling. Their staff specialise in drug and alcohol addiction, nothing else. Apparently, they're one of the top private clinics in the country, and they cost a fortune.'

'So, you think Jamie and his friend Carl Ashton were supplying, and Natalie was buying as well as Giles Stockton?' said Carys.

'No way. That was a lot of cocaine they were smuggling into the country,' said Barnes. 'More than two people would ever need.'

'Not if Natalie was selling it on to contacts she made through her job in the City,' said Gavin.

Kay leaned against Sharp's desk and handed Gavin's notes back to him. 'Good work, Piper. I think you might be onto something here, but we're going to have to proceed *very* carefully.' She cast her eyes over the assembled team. 'News about this development doesn't leave this room until the facts have been fully substantiated, is that understood?'

A murmured response reached her ears.

'Okay. Next steps. We don't want to alert Natalie Stockton to the fact that we've found out about this. Gavin's speculating that she may have had a cocaine addiction, that's all at the moment, so let's not get ahead of ourselves. Gav – can you phone the centre again and see if there's someone we can talk to this evening to establish the facts involving her stay?'

'Will do.'

He pulled out his mobile phone and retreated to a corner of the room, speaking in a hushed tone.

'Ian, I'll need you to cover for these two while we're working through Gavin's theory. What's your workload like at the moment?'

'Not too bad. I can take on the community policing thing Carys was going to attend in the morning at HQ – it's only a meet and greet, anyway. What else do you want to throw my way?'

'Piper was supposed to be finalising a report for the CPS about Carl Ashton. It's all written; I won't have time to review it before it goes over to Jude Martin, that's all.'

'Leave it with me.'

'Thanks.'

She paused as Gavin shoved his phone in his pocket and wandered over.

'I spoke with the receptionist,' he said. 'None of the counsellors are around at the moment, and she won't release any information to me without checking with them first. She sounds like she's only about eighteen, so she's probably erring on the side of caution rather than being deliberately obstructive. On the upside, she has confirmed the name of one of the counsellors who was there ten years ago, and even went so far as to make an appointment for me to speak with him in the morning. Bloke by the name of Zack Ellington.'

'Brilliant, that's great. All right – Carys, I'll need you to find out the name of Natalie's employers in the City from ten years ago. If they're not mentioned in any of the statements, then check her social media. Carefully, mind. Set up an appointment for us to meet with someone there tomorrow if you can. And, if they give you any trouble about it, remind them we're dealing with a murder investigation here.'

'Got it.'

'Okay, that's enough for one day. It's late, so clear off and get some rest. I've got a feeling we're going to be busy for the next few days.'

FORTY-TWO

Kay peered out of the rain-lashed train window and rested her chin in her hand as the Kentish countryside turned to urban sprawl.

She wouldn't admit it to anyone, but she worried that she hadn't told Sharp about the breakthrough in their investigation. Part of her felt obliged to keep him up to date about progress, but her conscience wrestled with the fact that he was so closely connected to the Ingrams.

How on earth was she supposed to inform any of them that Natalie could have been Jamie's buyer?

'Here you go.'

She turned at the sound of Carys's voice, and then took the cup of coffee she held out with a smile of thanks.

'You were miles away,' said the young DC. She slid into the seat opposite Kay and placed her own cup on the table between them. 'What were you thinking about?'

'I'm kicking myself for not considering that Natalie could be the buyer before now. The other part of me is wondering how on earth I'm going to tell her parents if we're right.'

'Do you think Gavin is onto something?'

Kay shrugged, and took a sip of her coffee before wrinkling her nose.

'Sorry,' said Carys. 'They only had decaf.'

'It's okay. I'll live. I think he is, yes. Unless Zack Ellington can confirm that at the time Natalie was residing at the clinic they were offering grief counselling as part of their programme, then I think we need to seriously consider the fact she could have had an addiction and was using her brother to obtain the drugs she craved. Like I said last night though, we have to approach this a step at a time – we can't assume anything.'

The train began to slow, and Carys glanced out of the window as the sign for Herne Hill station came into view. She glanced at her watch, and sighed.

'Good job the only appointment they offered us

was for eleven o'clock. Any earlier, and we would have been late the way this train is running.'

Kay smiled, and pushed her coffee cup away, unable to stomach any more of the foul-tasting liquid. 'I can't remember the last time I came up to London. Before everything happened to me, and before Adam's veterinary practice became so successful, we used to try and get up here once a month.'

'Did you go to the theatre to see a show or something like that?'

'No – and this is going to sound really boring, but we used to like wandering around people watching and finding interesting bars tucked out of the way to have a drink in. I think it was more about the change of scenery than anything else.' She reached out and used her paper napkin to wipe condensation from the window. 'I couldn't live there though. I'm definitely a country person.'

'Me too. Last time I was here was to go to an exhibition at the V&A six months ago.'

Kay's phone vibrated in her bag, and she fished it out, inwardly groaning as she read the text message.

'What's the matter?'

'Nothing. It's Sharp, wanting an update.'

'What are you going to tell him?'

'Nothing. If I have anything to report, I'll do it

when we have all the facts, and I'll speak to him face to face.'

She shoved the phone back into her bag as an announcement came over the intercom, advising passengers the train would soon be entering Victoria Station.

Carys began to gather up her things. 'We can walk to the office from the station. It's only about five minutes from there.'

Kay peered out of the window at the dark clouds hovering ominously above the city before the train slid under the roof of the station and ground to a halt.

'Hopefully we won't drown before we arrive.'

FORTY-THREE

The skyscraper that held the financial institution where Natalie Stockton had once worked was a glass-covered edifice that contrasted starkly with the Regency buildings on the opposite side of the street.

Kay led the way past an automatic sliding door and into an expansive reception area that resembled a five-star hotel rather than a private business.

A crimson-coloured carpet lined the floor and deadened their footsteps as they approached the reception desk, one that she noted with surprise had been carved from a single tree before its surface had then been varnished to a high sheen.

The same effect could be said of the woman sitting behind it.

She wore a headset over a coiffed hair style, her

bright pink nail lacquer flashing under the overhead spotlights as she directed a call. As Kay and Carys approached, she continued talking on the phone, gestured to a leather-bound visitor's book, and indicated that they should both sign in.

That done, the woman finished the call and smiled.

'Can I ask who you're here to see?'

'Marion Wisehart,' said Carys.

'Take a seat, please. I'll let her know you're here.'

'Remind me who this Marion Wisehart is?' said Kay as they sat.

'HR Manager – or "People Management Specialist" as she informed me late yesterday,' said Carys, barely concealing her amusement at the title. 'Sounded okay on the phone. Guarded, yes, but—'

'Understandable, given she has to protect the reputation of the business.'

'Exactly.'

Kay turned her attention to a door that opened next to the receptionist, and a woman of about fifty appeared, her light brown hair cut into a fashionable style that left it long at the front and short at the back.

Large earrings sparkled and accentuated her long neck, and she wore a crisp charcoal-coloured suit.

Kay and Carys rose as she neared and introduced themselves to Marion Wisehart.

'Detective Hunter? I understand from my conversation with your colleague here that this couldn't be dealt with via a phone call?'

'Probably best if we chat face to face.'

'All right. Come on through.'

She turned and led the way across the reception area, swiped her security card over the door lock, and then paused to usher them into an open plan office that hummed with proficiency.

Rows of desks lined the floor; a person sat at each with a headset on and conversing in muted tones while computer screens flickered before their eyes.

The whole effect was one of a busy hive.

Wisehart ignored the throng of employees, and turned right before opening a door and flicking on a light switch.

Kay stepped into what resembled a square box, a small table and chairs in the centre and frosted glass separating it from the central workspace. Whiteboard markers had been used to scribble on the glass, and she noticed Wisehart's top lip curl when she closed the door.

'Really,' she said with an exasperated sigh, 'they

know they're supposed to wipe down the walls when they're finished.'

'What's this room used for?' said Carys.

'We encourage our employees to brainstorm any issues before raising them with management,' said Wisehart, taking a bright coloured cloth from a cabinet at the back of the room and attacking the scrawl until it faded. 'We tested it for three months and found a twenty per cent decrease in our managers' time being used to sort out minor problems. They've got more important things to do, believe me.'

Kay gave a slight shake of her head as she caught Carys's eyes glazing over, and they each took a seat at the table.

'Right,' said Wisehart, tossing the cloth back into the cabinet and joining them. 'You mentioned on the phone that you wanted to talk about Natalie Ingram. You do understand I can only give you information that isn't deemed confidential?'

Kay smiled and leaned forward as Carys opened her notebook. 'That's fair enough, Ms Wisehart, but so *you* understand – I'm currently leading an investigation into a potential murder, and so I do expect you to give me your full cooperation.'

'Oh. Oh, I see.' The woman's eyes widened for a

moment before she recovered and lowered her voice. 'How can I help?'

'First of all, I have to insist that this conversation is treated with confidence,' said Kay. 'We're conducting some preliminary enquiries at the present time, although if we need to, we will seek full disclosure for Natalie's personnel file. Can you tell me when Natalie started working here?'

'About thirteen years ago,' said Wisehart. 'She'd finished university and demonstrated a knack for being extremely hard working and diligent during a temporary position here after graduating. We find a lot of our best employees that way – to be honest, it saves a lot of hassle offering permanent contracts with probationary periods, only to discover that after the initial three months, staff slacken off, and you're stuck with them. We offer six-month temporary contracts – gives us a better idea of whether people are right for us.'

'And how long did Natalie work here?'

'She left after two years.' Wisehart lowered her gaze. 'I felt terrible, really I did, when I heard that her brother had been killed six weeks after we terminated her contract.'

Kay tensed. 'We were under the impression that Natalie quit work after her brother died.'

Wisehart choked out a bitter laugh. 'Natalie Ingram didn't quit, Detective Hunter. She was fired.'

'Why?'

'You have to understand that this is off the record. I'll deny it if I'm asked.'

'We'll seek the necessary authorities if we want to take this further with you.'

Wisehart took a deep breath, and then rested her hands on the table. 'Look, we had a few instances with Natalie when she'd turn up late – mid-morning, not just ten minutes here and there. Her work became sloppy, and there were a couple of occasions where she could've cost this firm millions of pounds because her mind wasn't on the job. She pushed her luck – despite formal warnings, it happened again. We had to let her go.'

'What was wrong with her? Was she sick or something?'

'No. Sky-high on something. Cocaine, I suspect, although we could never prove anything. Natalie Ingram was rather too fond of burning the candle at both ends, Detective.'

FORTY-FOUR

Kay and Carys had reached Maidstone by mid-afternoon, and after leaving the detective constable to type up her report from their meeting that morning, Kay signalled to Gavin and grabbed her bag.

'Where are we going?' he said.

'To the Ingrams' house. I want to ask them some questions about Natalie, and I want to do it face to face.'

He followed her downstairs, signed out for a pool vehicle, and then led the way out to the car park.

As he shifted gears and steered the vehicle through the busy town centre, Kay flipped through her notebook.

'How did you get on talking to Zack Ellington?'

'He confirmed they don't offer grief counselling – never have. They specialise in addiction, including drugs and alcohol. Obviously, he wouldn't confirm if Natalie Ingram had ever been a patient there, but he said he would help us further if we got the appropriate paperwork for him. Their basic programme is for six weeks, and they charged two thousand quid per week back then, which only included the counselling sessions. Accommodation and food were extra charges.'

Kay brought him up to speed on what she had discovered at Natalie's ex-employers that morning, and he gave a low whistle under his breath.

'So, she was the buyer.'

Kay bumped her fist against the door, and tried to sort her thoughts into a coherent sequence.

'There's one thing that doesn't make sense though – Carl Ashton said that that half a kilo was the least they'd smuggled in. Okay, we might have circumstantial evidence to suggest that Natalie was a user, but how on earth was she financing the purchase of that much cocaine?'

She fell silent, an idea tugging at her memory, and tried to grasp at it. She held a finger to her lips to stop Gavin interrupting, and closed her eyes.

The conversation she had had with Penny Boyd was going around in her mind, and then she realised with a start what was bothering her.

'Gav? When Barnes and I first spoke with Michael and Bridget Ingram to let them know we were reopening the investigation into Jamie's death, Michael said that Jamie had received a phone call late that night before he stormed out of the house to answer it. He left the house soon after that. But when we spoke with Penny Boyd, she said that she had phoned Jamie just after the Ingrams had had dinner.'

Gavin remained silent for a moment, navigating across a roundabout, and then Kay saw realisation cross his features.

'Jamie Ingram received *two* phone calls that night, not just the one his parents knew about. So, who was the second caller?'

Kay closed her notebook. 'Okay, we speak to the Ingrams to see what we can find out about Natalie's work, and then we formally interview her.'

'Do you think she was acting as an intermediary? Do you think something went wrong and it got Jamie killed by the people she was selling to?'

'Maybe. I don't know – it feels like we're close, but we're only hearing half the story.'

Gavin slowed the car as he turned into the farmyard, and parked next to the front door.

Kay emitted a surprised grunt as she saw the vehicle parked over by the barn. 'Looks like we won't have to go over to Yalding to speak with Natalie. That's her car.'

Michael Ingram answered the door with a glass of wine in his hand. His smile faded as he took in the two police detectives on his doorstep.

'Kay? What's going on?'

'Can we come in? It's quite urgent that I speak with you.'

'Of course. We were just washing up.'

They made their way through to the kitchen, where Bridget was up to her elbows in soap suds. Her face clouded as they entered the room, and she plucked a towel from the worktop and dried her hands.

'Did you want a coffee or something?' said Michael.

Kay shook her head. 'Is Natalie here?'

'Not at the moment.'

'Oh. Look, in her absence – can you tell me when she left her job in the City?'

Michael scratched his chin. 'About six months after Jamie died, I think. She came out of counselling for her grief, tried to get back into the swing of things, but said she found it too stressful, so she quit. She met Giles soon after that.'

'Did you ever go to her office in the City?'

'No. Why would we?'

'Bridget, on the night Jamie died, what time did you say he received that phone call?'

'It was late, and we were watching a film. The ones that come on after the nine o'clock news, so I supposed it was about half ten?'

'And did he say who the caller was?'

'No.'

'Can you excuse me for a moment?'

Kay pushed her chair back and strode back out to the hallway, thumbing through her phone until she found the number she wanted, then dialled it and crossed her fingers.

A whispered voice answered. 'Hello?'

'Penny Boyd? It's DI Hunter.'

'I'm at work at the moment. I can't talk.'

'It's urgent. You said you phoned Jamie Ingram the night of his death. Can you recall the time?'

'The time?'

'Yes. The time you phoned him that night. What was it?'

'Um, they'd finished dinner, I think. Jamie was

really annoyed because I phoned when they were washing up, and he had to step out into the yard to speak with me.'

'Thanks, Mrs Boyd.'

'Is everything all right?' Bridget's eyes were wide as Kay walked back into the kitchen and tucked her phone into her bag before picking up her notebook.

Gavin remained silent, having worked with her long enough to know when her thoughts were operating in overdrive.

She flicked through the pages, and felt her heart sink as she reread her hurried scrawl.

'Whose idea was it to throw away Jamie's phone?'

'We didn't throw it away,' said Bridget. 'I told you – we gave it to one of those phone recycling charities. Something "ark".'

'Whose idea was it to do that?'

'Natalie's,' said Michael. 'What's going on, Kay?'

'Did you ever meet Giles before Jamie's death?'

'No.'

'Where is Natalie?'

'She's gone – we had a lovely surprise this morning; the girl that Jamie was seeing when he was in the army came to visit us. We thought it would be nice for her and Natalie to meet, so we phoned Nat to get her to come over and we organised lunch.'

'We hadn't met her before,' said Bridget, wiping at her eyes. 'Lovely girl. Has kids of her own now. She'd have made Jamie very happy.'

'Oh, I don't know,' said Michael. 'She was okay when she first got here, but she seemed to get nervous when Natalie turned up. Jamie was so gregarious and full of life – it's hard to imagine him with her.'

'Where are Amber and Natalie right now?' said Kay.

'Natalie asked Amber to drive her home,' Michael said. 'Natalie reckoned she'd had too much to drink, and so suggested she leave her car here, and that Amber drive her back to Yalding. I was a bit surprised, actually. I only saw Nat drink one glass of wine. What's going on?'

Kay didn't answer him. Instead, she grabbed Gavin by the arm and propelled him towards the front door, pulling out her mobile phone and dialling Amber Fitzroy's number.

She cursed as it went to voicemail.

'What's wrong, guv?'

'There's no answer.' Her skin crawled, and a sinking sensation twisted at her stomach. 'Gav, phone for back-up. I want a uniformed patrol here as soon as possible. Nobody leaves until I say so. We're going to the Stocktons' house. Use the lights and siren, and have another patrol car meet us there.'

FORTY-FIVE

'Shit, she *used* us.'

'Guv?'

Kay hung on to the strap above the passenger window of the car as Gavin swung the vehicle around the narrow country lanes, and gasped as they shot across a T-junction, a tractor braking at the last minute to avoid the collision.

'Sorry, guv.' He eased his foot off the accelerator, then glanced at Kay. 'What's going on?'

'I think Amber Fitzroy knew about Natalie's drug addiction, and possibly Giles's connection to Jamie's smuggling operation, and was psyching herself up to tell Michael and Bridget. I don't think she expected Michael to insist on Natalie being at the farmhouse to meet her, and it didn't give her time to speak to them alone. Michael had a fair point – Amber does come across as being quite reserved, and it may have been the case that she was reluctant to broach the subject as soon as she arrived there.'

Kay pulled out her mobile phone and scrolled through the recent calls list until she found the number she needed.

It went straight to voicemail.

'Dammit. Giles Stockton isn't answering.'

'Do you think Natalie viewed Amber as a threat?'

'I do, yes. She's the only one in the family that knew about her, but didn't know her name.'

'But, why?'

'Think about it. Natalie's spent years cultivating a perfect persona in front of her family. She lied about losing her job in the City; she lied about her cocaine habit – even going as far as booking herself into a rehab clinic several miles away where she wasn't known by anyone. She's obviously never told her parents what she and Jamie were up to. Then, Amber turns up out of the blue. The one person Natalie has had no control over – until now.'

'So, she's been using our cold case investigation to find out who she is, and where she is, in order to flush her out and keep her quiet, you mean?'

'Exactly. It's only a guess, but I think Amber must

have let slip that she had spoken to the police, and that's why she's here in Kent. Natalie might have got paranoid about what was said when we interviewed her. You heard what Michael said. Amber clammed up when Natalie appeared—'

Kay turned her attention to her phone as it began to ring.

'Kay? It's Carys. The patrol car is a couple of minutes behind you. The other two have arrived at the Ingrams' farmhouse – Natalie and Amber haven't returned there.'

'Thanks. Keep me posted. We're nearly in Yalding.'

Gavin cursed under his breath as he steered the vehicle around a tight right-hand bend, straightening the car before taking a sharp left.

Using the back roads to reach the Stocktons' house was a more direct route than going through Maidstone, but Kay noticed the detective constable's knuckles were white as he gripped the steering wheel.

'We're nearly there,' she said. 'The turning for Vicarage Lane is down here on the left.'

She dug her toes into the foot well to steady herself as Gavin shifted down a gear and took the corner without slowing down.

'Have you been taking driving lessons from Barnes?'

'How did you guess?'

Kay gritted her teeth.

Less than a minute later, the vehicle slid to a standstill on the gravel outside the Stocktons' house.

Kay threw herself out of the car and raced across to the front door, hammering on its surface as Gavin joined her.

'Dammit.' She took a step back and peered up at the windows facing the driveway. 'Gav – get yourself around the back of the house. See if there's a way in – or if someone's already left that way.'

'Guv.'

His boots sent loose gravel flying into the air as he tore past her and disappeared from sight.

She moved closer to the ground floor window of Natalie's office and shielded her eyes from the weak sunlight that reflected off the glass.

Inside, the room was empty, with no sign of Natalie, or Amber.

Gavin returned a moment later, a key in his hand. 'No-one's gone out that way – it's blocked off with a wheelie bin. I found a key under a flowerpot, though.'

She glanced over her shoulder as a patrol car slid

to a halt behind Gavin's vehicle, and two uniformed officers hurried towards them.

Kay walked over to meet them as they approached. 'We believe Amber Fitzroy's life is in danger and she may be held in the Stocktons' house against her will. Piper's found a spare key, so in the circumstances, I'm taking the decision to go in. I want you two to stay out here. If anyone turns up, yell.'

'Guv.'

She followed Gavin as he made his way around the building, and then pulled the wheelie bin out of the way and extracted his telescopic night stick as he opened the door.

'Natalie?'

The house remained silent in response.

Kay pulled out two pairs of disposable gloves from her pocket and tossed one pair to Gavin. 'Okay, you take upstairs, I'll stay down here.'

She followed him into the hallway, then moved through the living room door at the foot of the staircase as he climbed from view.

Thick rugs lined a slate floor, a large television hanging on the far wall in front of a wraparound sofa. Strategically placed cushions covered alternate seats, and a wooden toy chest sat beside it.

An open magazine lay discarded on a coffee table next to a half-empty mug of coffee.

Gavin appeared at the door. 'Upstairs is clear – no sign of her.'

'Let's see what's in her office.' Her phone began to ring, and she saw Giles Stockton's number displayed. 'Thanks for phoning back.'

'What do you want, Detective? I'm not talking to you without my solicitor being—'

'Shut up and listen, Giles. Where's Natalie?'

'What the hell is going on?'

'When was the last time you saw your wife?'

'This morning, when I left for work.'

'Your wife isn't at the house. Where else might she be? Do you own any other houses?'

'What? What are you doing in my house? How dare—'

'Do you own any other property?'

'With the size of our mortgage? Of course we bloody don't.'

'A woman's life may be in danger. Where else might Natalie be?'

'She'll be collecting the kids from day care. The centre closes soon, and they charge extra if we're late.'

'Which one?'

Kay hung up after Stockton had given her the details, and hurried outside. She handed the scrawled note to one of the uniformed officers. 'Get onto them and find out if Natalie Stockton showed up to collect her kids. Let me know what you find out.'

She ran back inside, and caught up with Gavin in Natalie's office.

'She must've taken Amber somewhere else. Giles confirmed they don't own any other property, and I'm sure Natalie is paranoid about what she thinks Amber might know. We have to hurry, Gav. I think Amber's in danger.'

'The notes on the database say that when you and Barnes first spoke with Natalie, she was working on two commissions.'

'Right – rental properties were one of her specialities, she said. So, somewhere in here, there's a note of where Amber might be.'

'What do you think happened?'

'Maybe it was Natalie who called Jamie late that night. I don't think she knew that her future husband and brother knew each other – I think she was worried Jamie was going to tell their parents about her drug habit.'

'But surely, she could have simply counter-threatened him with the supply chain he had set up?'

'Not if she knew he'd told Amber he was planning to end it, and report it to his commanding officer two days later. He had nothing to lose. But what if Natalie panicked? She was an addict; she was about to lose her supply, and their parents would find out.'

'How does that tie in with Jamie's death?'

'I don't know.'

She turned as one of the uniformed officers entered the room, his hand on his radio.

'We've heard from the car sent to the childcare centre, guv. No sign of Natalie Stockton. Both her kids are still there. We've made arrangements for them to be looked after until we find their mother.'

'Thank you.'

'Guv – I think I've got something here.'

She moved back to the desk where Gavin was sifting through a sheaf of pages. He handed one to her as she joined him.

'This is one of her commissions. It's for a rental property over at Windmill Hill. The tenants moved out two weeks ago, and the photography session for the rental agent isn't due until two days' time. She's got the key while she sorts out all the furniture and everything to stage the rooms.'

'Let's go.' She paused at the door and turned to

the uniformed officer. 'Stay here. If Natalie Stockton turns up, don't let her disappear again. Gav – with me.'

They dashed to the car, Gavin flooring the accelerator as Kay clipped her seatbelt into place.

'What about Harrison? Where does he fit into all of this?' he said.

'Maybe he realised that if Jamie's death was properly investigated the way Sharp wanted it, he'd be exposed for dropping the cannabis possession charges against Giles.'

'But then why make accusations against Sharp that he was covering this up?'

'Because his career is over, Gav – and he wants to take down Sharp with him, or at least discredit him in any way he could so that no-one would believe Sharp's accusations against him.'

'If Natalie knew Harrison was involved in her husband's charges being dropped, why didn't she say anything?'

'Perhaps she was too scared.'

'So, what's changed?'

'I don't know. I hope to hell we're not too late, and we get the chance to ask her.'

FORTY-SIX

As Gavin drove towards Windmill Hill, Kay scanned the pages from Natalie's notes regarding the property, and then cursed under her breath.

'There's no phone number for the agent, and I can't get a signal for my phone apps.'

'Wait until we pass Mereworth – the signal will be better by the time we get to the top of Seven Mile Lane.'

'I bloody hope so.'

Kay folded the pages, the content committed to memory.

A two-bedroom Victorian end-of-terrace, the rental property was expected to attract a significant number of interested buyers now that its tenants had moved out, which was why the owners had opted to have the whole place staged with Natalie's interior design skills. She had been tasked with sourcing furniture, artwork, and other bric-à-brac to bring out the best in the home in order to help secure the highest price possible. Her fee for this, in Kay's opinion, was extortionate.

She hoped for the owners' sake they got a good price.

Gavin indicated left, tore along a straight narrow lane, and then accelerated past a Georgian farmhouse that displayed signs inviting the public to visit its ornate Italian gardens. He slowed for a sharp right-hand turn, and braked.

'This is Windmill Hill.'

'Okay. The rental property is about halfway down on the left. See if you can park before we get to it, and we'll walk the rest of the way.'

'Guv? Can I make a suggestion?'

'Yes.'

'Natalie hasn't met me. She'll spot you a mile off, so why don't I have a walk past first, and see what I find before we go barging in there?'

Kay nodded. 'Don't hang about, Gavin. We might not have much time.'

He spun on his heel and took off at a jog, slowing as he approached the row of houses.

Kay moved to the grass verge, out of the way of any passing traffic, and craned her neck to watch as the detective constable ambled past the terraced cottages as if out for a stroll.

Luckily, he was wearing a leather jacket over his suit and tie, and with his blonde hair sticking up in unruly tufts from time spent surfing, he didn't draw untoward attention.

She hoped.

He disappeared from view over the brow of the hill, returning five minutes later, and breaking into a run once he'd passed the house.

'No sign of anyone inside,' he said, joining her on the verge and turning back to face the terrace. 'There appears to be one bedroom at the front, and a living area below that – the front door opens straight into it, I would think. The curtains to the bedroom are closed.'

'Hiding something, do you think?'

'Or someone, perhaps. There's a phone number on the "For Sale" sign in the front garden,' he said, and recited it for her.

'Good work,' she said, as she waited for the call to be answered.

'Hodges and Wilkes Agents, can I help you?' a male voice said.

'Who am I speaking to?'

'Howard Wilkes, the owner. Who's this?'

'This is Detective Inspector Kay Hunter of Kent Police. Do you have a spare key at the property you're currently advertising for sale on Windmill Hill?'

'Why?'

'A woman's life may be in danger. I can either open the front door with a key, or have one of my officers use a battering ram, Mr Wilkes. I don't have time to mess around.'

'There's a loose patio tile – fourth one from the right as you're facing the back door. The key's underneath it.'

'Thank you.'

'What's going on, Detective?'

Kay ended the call, having no time to explain herself to the property agent. 'All right, Gav. Let's stick together this time, shall we?'

He gave her a grim smile. 'Sounds good to me. Back door?'

'Yeah. Let's go.'

They took off at a sprint, Gavin's longer legs putting him out in front within seconds.

He vaulted the garden gate, Kay opting to open it

rather than trip and fall, before hurrying down the side of the cottage in his wake.

By the time she reached the back garden, he was already crouching next to the patio, lifting the paving slab the agent had indicated.

The cottage had been extended at the back, a wrap-around conservatory now adding another dimension to the original kitchen floorplan, and Kay peered through the windows.

Nothing moved.

'Got it,' said Gavin, launching himself at the back door.

Kay extended her baton, and nodded. 'Do it.'

The key turned with ease, and Kay noted that the door sported a new lock, no doubt replaced by the agent to ensure previous tenants could no longer enter the property. The door opened without a squeak, and they eased into the light space.

Natalie's skill as an interior designer was apparent.

Indoor plants had been strategically placed around the conservatory, hugging the low walls under the windows without encroaching on two armchairs that sat side by side in such a way as to give the impression that the owners took their morning coffee ritual on a regular basis.

Magazines had been placed on an ornamental glass table, and as Kay moved into the kitchen, she sniffed the air.

A faint trace of vanilla clung to the walls.

'Perfume?' said Gavin in a low voice.

Kay shook her head. 'It's an old trick. Put a vanilla pod in the oven and warm it up before a viewing – makes the place smell like you've been baking, so it feels homely. They've obviously had a viewing within the past day or so.'

'Oh.'

After checking the bathroom, which like many Victorian houses was downstairs, Kay and Gavin moved to the right of the kitchen, passed through a small dining area and into the living room.

Again, Natalie's handiwork transformed the space into one of domestic bliss.

Pine cones had been stacked in the fire grate, while next to it a pile of logs had been placed next to an iron poker hanging from a rack. The two sofas had cushions piled on them, the bright colours a stark contrast to the muted tones of the walls.

However, there was no sign of Natalie – or Amber.

'Where are they?' said Gavin.

'Okay, let's check upstairs.'

Kay made her way out to the dining room. A door had been constructed in the left-hand wall to hide the staircase, and she rested her hand on it a moment, listening.

Then she wrenched it open, and called up the stairs.

'Natalie? Are you here? It's Kay Hunter.'

A dull *thud* reached her ears, and she glanced over her shoulder at Gavin.

'What was that?' he said.

In response, she raised her baton and charged up the stairs.

At the top step, she was faced with two doors – both closed.

She shoved open the one to her left, and discovered a single bed and nightstand, the back window providing a view over a long winding garden that led down to a footpath and, beyond that, a golf course.

She turned on the threshold, and saw Gavin had his hand on the door to the main bedroom.

'Go.'

He pushed open the door, and Kay barrelled into him.

He stepped to one side, and as she peered around his shoulder, she saw why he'd stopped so suddenly.

Amber Fitzroy sat on a chair next to the window, her wrists and ankles bound, and a gag that had been tied so tight across her mouth, she was having difficulty breathing.

Her eyes widened at the sight of the two detectives.

Kay breathed a sigh of relief as tears streaked down the woman's cheeks.

FORTY-SEVEN

Gavin found a knife in an ornamental block in the kitchen and slit the gag away from Amber's mouth, then placed his hand on her shoulder as she gulped in deep breaths.

'I thought she was going to kill me,' she gasped.

Gavin glanced over his shoulder at Kay. 'There's another knife missing from the block.'

Kay began to search the room, then crouched onto the rug that had been laid across the polished wooden floorboards and peered under the bed.

'Got it.' She dropped the bedclothes back into place; there was no sense in distressing the woman further, and they would retrieve the knife later. 'Where's Natalie?'

'She's gone,' said Amber, while Gavin began to loosen the bindings at her wrists and ankles.

'Did she say where she was going?'

'No – she kept saying it was all my fault, that if Jamie hadn't fallen in love with me, he would have been more careful hiding the drugs. She said that if I hadn't given the earrings back, he wouldn't have had second thoughts.'

'Why did you agree to leave the farm with her?'

'She said she wanted to talk, that's all. I believed her.' Fresh tears welled in her eyes. 'I can't believe I was so stupid. Oh my God, I really thought she was going to kill me.'

'Why did she want to bring you here?'

Confusion flittered across Amber's face. 'This is her house. She said she wanted me to meet her husband and kids.'

Kay exchanged a look with Gavin, then crouched down next to Amber and reached out for her hand. 'This isn't Natalie's house, Amber. This is an empty property that she helped to style while the owners are trying to sell it. No-one lives here.'

A shudder ran through the woman's body, and she gripped Kay's fingers. 'She brought me here on purpose?'

Kay nodded. 'I think so.'

The woman's pallor whitened even further. 'Oh my God.'

'Do you have any idea why she would attack you now?'

Amber rubbed at her wrists where the rope had dug into her skin. 'I think she panicked – she wasn't acting rationally after we'd left the farmhouse. At first, I took pity on her. That's why I agreed to give her a lift. I thought it'd give us a chance to talk about Jamie away from her parents.'

Gavin pulled a clean paper tissue from his jacket pocket and handed it to her, and they waited while she tried to compose herself.

'When we got here, she was going on about how happy she was that I'd get to meet her kids – everything was normal until we got up here. She said they were playing in that other room, but as I was following her up the stairs, I thought it was weird that I couldn't hear anything. You know what kids are like when they're playing – it's usually bedlam.' She shook her head. 'I was so stupid to believe her.'

'What did she do?'

Amber rubbed at the goose bumps that were forming on her arms. 'The moment we reached the top of the stairs, she changed. We struggled; she overpowered me – it was as if she had something like this planned all along.'

'Did she say why she assaulted you?

'It turns out she thought Jamie had told me she was involved with the drug smuggling all those years ago, that I had told you, and had planned to tell her parents. I had no idea she was selling the drugs for Jamie until she told me when we got here. She was pacing up and down waving that knife in front of me.' A sob escaped her lips. 'When I said I didn't have a clue what she was going on about, she got confused and started muttering to herself, and that's when she took my car keys and left.'

Kay placed a hand on Amber's shoulder. 'You're safe now. Gavin will take care of you. We'll need to get a formal statement from you, too.'

Amber sniffed, then nodded, colour returning to her features. 'Okay.'

'Where are you going, guv?' Gavin moved towards her.

'Stay here. I'll get Carys to catch up with me. I need to find Natalie.'

FORTY-EIGHT

Kay spun the wheel and eased the car over the cattle grid that separated the Ingrams' farm from the lane. A smudge of bright blue had caught her eye in the rear-view mirror, and she breathed a sigh of relief as Carys braked to a standstill beside her in another pool car.

They'd spoken on the phone while Kay had manoeuvred her way across the busy Maidstone ring road, and arranged to meet at the farm.

It was the only logical place Kay could think to start.

'What do you reckon?' said Carys. She leaned against the back door of Kay's vehicle and stared up at the farmhouse. 'Think she's back here?'

'Her car's here. No sign of Amber's vehicle though, so I don't know – unless she's parked it somewhere else?' She moved away from the vehicle and surveyed the surrounding orchards. 'I thought she might come back here. It's a place she thinks of as safe. It's where she and Jamie grew up, after all, and Bridget said they were always close.'

The front door opened, and Michael Ingram peered out.

'Kay? What's going on?'

Kay squared her shoulders, and strode over to where he stood. 'We think Natalie and Amber had a disagreement. Did Natalie come back here?'

'No. What sort of disagreement?'

'I'll explain later. Right now, my priority is to find Natalie. Did she and Jamie have a special hiding place, or somewhere they used to go when they were younger? Somewhere they could play away from the house, for instance?'

Bridget appeared, her face lined with worry. 'Kay? Where's Natalie and Amber?'

'Amber's okay. We're trying to ascertain whether Natalie has an old childhood hiding place here on the farm. Somewhere she might go if she needed to feel safe. Any ideas?'

The woman's brow creased, and then her eyes lit up. 'There's an old chestnut tree at the bottom of the apple orchard on the far boundary to the farm.' She pointed past Kay, and beyond the barn. 'She and Jamie got Michael to put up a swing when they were about eight years old – we used to lose them for hours down there.'

'How do we reach it?'

'There's a footpath that runs past the barn, then down towards a stream. That's our boundary. The apple orchard is on your right. You'll find a stile in the hedgerow as the path ends – you can get into the orchard that way.'

Michael moved away from the door, then returned with an old green anorak clutched in his hands. 'I'm coming with you.'

'I need you to stay there.'

'But I can help. I need to know she's okay.'

'And I need you and Bridget to be at home in case she comes back here. Please, Michael. Let me deal with this.'

He acquiesced with a sigh, and Kay spun away from the doorstep.

She and Carys ran over to the barn, startling a small flock of chickens that pecked at the ground in search of food before flapping away from the two women as they approached.

Thick mud slapped against Kay's boots as she led

the way, the path too narrow for them to traverse it side by side.

They remained silent, each lost in their own thoughts as Kay's eyes swept the landscape to her right, desperate to find Natalie.

Gnarled tree trunks grew in rows, with bare branches twisted and grey against a backdrop of sparse hedgerows and sodden earth. The grass in the orchard had been left longer over the winter months while the farm retreated into a maintenance routine ready for the spring.

Kay tried to imagine the fields exploding with pink and white blossom, but the bleak vista clouded her imagination and darkened her thoughts.

If Natalie was as unstable as she feared, then she had to prepare herself for the worst.

She slowed her pace as the stile in the hedgerow came into view, and placed her finger on her lips.

Carys nodded, and lowered her voice.

'Can you see her?'

Kay climbed onto the footplate of the stile and cast her eyes around the orchard. She swore under her breath. 'What the hell does a chestnut tree look like in the winter? I can't remember.'

'Well, it'll be bigger than these,' said Carys. 'Bridget

said it was right on their boundary, didn't she? If I was a kid, I'd want a swing next to the stream, so I could dam that if I got bored. That's what me and my cousin used to do whenever we were out in the countryside.'

Kay managed a smile. 'Good thinking. Come on.'

They trudged across the orchard, and as the apple trees began to thin out, Kay noticed that natural woodland had been left to encroach upon the property.

A flash of red caught her eye, and she grabbed hold of Carys's sleeve.

'There.'

As she watched, the red moved in an arc, left to right, left to right, and she realised what she was looking at.

'It's Natalie. Bridget was right – she's on the swing.'

'What do you want to do, guv?'

'Stay here.'

Kay didn't wait for a response. She moved forward until she was within Natalie's line of vision, and then tucked her hands in her pockets and tried to look relaxed.

The swing moved back and forth under Natalie's guidance, her denim-clad legs pushing the air. Her head drooped to her chest, and as Kay drew closer she saw the vacant expression on the woman's face.

'Natalie? It's Kay Hunter. Are you okay?'

The woman's eyes widened as her head jerked up, and she froze.

Kay kept her voice steady, and tried to ignore the sound of blood rushing in her ears. Her heart hammered painfully, and she took a deep breath.

'What are you doing out here?'

'We used to argue about whose turn it was.'

Kay leaned against the trunk of the tree and cast her eyes over the mist that clung to the orchard as the swing slowed to a standstill.

'What happened, Natalie? How did Jamie die?'

'I just wanted to talk. He wouldn't listen to me.'

The woman began to sob, and Kay raised her arm, beckoning to Carys, before turning back to the woman.

'Come on, Natalie. We've got some talking to do, too.'

FORTY-NINE

Kay paced Sharp's office and nibbled at the ragged end of her thumbnail.

Debbie had shooed her from the incident room half an hour before, telling her she was distracting everyone else from their work, such was her inability to keep still while she awaited news.

She paused in front of the whiteboard, running over the facts in her mind, preparing herself for the psychological battle of wits that would commence within the hour, once the formal interviews began.

'Kay?'

She turned at the sound of Barnes's voice.

He stood on the threshold, his hand on the door.

'What's wrong?'

'Nothing – the car's here. They're bringing him into the interview room now.'

'They've kept them separated, yes?'

'Yes. All good.'

'Thanks. Let's go, then.'

Upon the arrest of Natalie Stockton, a phone call had been made to their counterparts in the Metropolitan Police to go to her husband's place of work and bring him back to Kent for questioning.

The Met had obliged, and to save time, a car from Kent Police had been sent to intercept them at Clacket Lane services on the M25, where Giles Stockton was transferred from one vehicle to the other and whisked along the M20 back to Maidstone.

As Kay left Sharp's office, she felt the weight of responsibility more than ever before.

Not only was she seeking justice for Jamie Ingram, but her colleagues were expecting her to uphold Sharp's reputation, too.

She followed Barnes along the corridor towards the stairs, and stopped when Larch appeared at his office door.

'I heard Giles and Natalie Stockton are in custody?'

'Yes, guv.'

'Take your time, Hunter. Make this count.'

'Guv.'

She hurried to catch up with Barnes, her hand on the smooth wooden surface of the banister as they descended to the ground floor, her copy of the investigation folder gripped within the other hand.

Although certain, she knew many questions remained unanswered, and she had to get it right. The slightest error would have devastating consequences.

Barnes used his swipe card to enter the interview suites, then stood with his hand hovering over the security panel to interview room one and turned to her, an eyebrow raised.

'Ready?'

'Ready.'

He swiped his card and pushed the door open, holding it for her as she followed him into the room.

The sweet tang of sweat and desperation assaulted her, and in that moment, she knew her instincts had been right.

Giles Stockton sat rigid in one of two plastic chairs on one side of the table in the middle of the room, his face grey.

The confident and indignant man she'd spoken to before was gone. Now she saw the hunted expression in his eyes as he watched her approach, and a fear she hadn't seen before.

Next to him, his solicitor capped and uncapped a fountain pen, the soft double *pop-pop* a nervous rhythm that accompanied Kay's footsteps on the tiled floor.

Barnes pulled out one of the spare chairs for her, then leaned across and started the recording equipment before lowering himself into the seat beside her.

He introduced himself and Kay for the purposes of the recording, stated the solicitor's and Stockton's names, and cited the formal caution.

Only then did he defer to Kay.

She was grateful to him. His years of experience meant that his actions had allowed her a few more moments to observe Stockton and gauge his mood, and she recalled Larch's words.

Make this count.

'When we first interviewed you, you stated that you met your wife Natalie at a party in Wateringbury two years after her brother, Jamie, died. Is there anything you would like to clarify or change in that statement?'

Stockton's gaze fell to his lap. 'I would. I met Natalie about eighteen months before her brother died.'

'Where did you meet her?'

'At a party in the City that the firm she worked for organised. It was to celebrate a major contract they had won, and because the bank I worked for help to finance it, some of us were invited as guests.'

'How would you describe your relationship at that time?'

He shrugged, and raised his head. 'We slept together from time to time, but it wasn't serious. Back then, it was a bit of fun.'

'How did you meet Jamie Ingram?'

'I told you the truth. I met him at a charity fundraiser at the Hop Farm.'

'Was this before or after you had started sleeping with his sister?'

'After. I only realised that after Jamie and I had been chatting for a while – I put two and two together, and told him I knew Nat.'

'When did the three of you come up with the idea of a cocaine smuggling operation?'

'It wasn't like that.'

Kay leaned back in her seat, and contemplated the man in front of her. 'Then perhaps you can enlighten me as to what it *was* like.'

Stockton ran a hand through his hair, his gaze travelling over the surface of the table. He licked his lips. 'That first time, Jamie confided in Natalie what he had done – stealing the drugs, I mean. He was panicking. Here he was with half a kilo of cocaine in his possession, and no idea what he was going to do with it. It was laughable really. You can imagine the lifestyle Natalie and I were living in London – we had high-pressure jobs, worked long hours, and partied as hard as we could. Natalie suggested to me that we could siphon off a little of the cocaine at a time, and sell it.'

'Are you suggesting it was Natalie's idea to sell the drugs?'

'Yes. She had most of the contacts to start with, after all. It's what I liked about her; she's always been outgoing, makes friends easily, and is great at networking.'

'How long did this go on for?'

'Up until that last lot got discovered in the container at the barracks.'

'Tell me about Simon Harrison,' said Kay.

Stockton visibly shuddered. 'I wish I'd never met the man.'

'What happened?'

'You know what happened,' he sneered. 'He got the charges against me dropped, and I got to keep my job.'

'In return for what?'

'A cut of our proceeds. I couldn't say "no", could I? I had student debts coming out of my ears after leaving university, I was trying to save some money for a house of my own, and I was one of the lucky few who still had a job after the banking crisis. Why the hell do you think Nat and I got involved in the first place?'

'Did you kill Jamie Ingram?' said Barnes. 'Did you and Carl Ashton decide you were better off without him? One less piece of the pie to share out?'

'No, dammit. I've told you before. I had nothing to do with Jamie's death.'

Kay leaned across the table and glared at Stockton. 'But you do know who was responsible, don't you, Giles?'

The man turned to his solicitor and muttered under his breath.

The solicitor blinked once, and then raised his gaze to Kay. 'I'd like a few moments with my client, Detective Hunter.'

FIFTY

Barnes leaned against the wall of the corridor between the doors to the interview rooms, and closed his eyes.

'They're a right pair, aren't they?'

'Yeah. You ready for the next one?'

He opened his eyes, then led the way into interview room three.

Natalie Stockton glared at them from her seat, her arms folded across her chest, her eyes swollen and red.

Kay nodded to the solicitor sitting beside her – she'd met him before, and knew how much his firm charged on an hourly rate.

She resisted the urge to sigh. Despite Michael and

Bridget's attempts to give their daughter the best legal counsel they could, it would have the same result.

She knew Natalie was guilty.

'Why did you get involved?'

'Jamie and I always did everything together,' said Natalie, dropping her arms to the table, a petulant expression clouding her features. 'You can ask Mum and Dad. Inseparable, everyone said. Then he joined the army, and everything changed. He made new friends, and I hardly saw him anymore. If he did come to the farm, we used to get visitors – his old friends, wanting to catch up with him, or people from the army. As if he didn't see enough of them. I caught them talking, him and Carl Ashton. Summer, it was. They'd been helping in the orchards. Afterwards, they were chatting over a beer. They didn't hear me approaching, but I heard what they were talking about. I told Jamie he had to include me.'

'Otherwise you'd report him.'

A malevolent gleam appeared in Natalie's eyes. 'Carl was pissed off, but Jamie agreed. He knew I meant it.'

'And Giles?'

Natalie snorted, and turned her gaze to the floor. 'Along for the ride. Honestly, if he'd never met Jamie and me, he'd have amounted to nothing.'

'Who were your buyers?'

'I can't tell you.'

Kay rested her hands on the table and waited until the woman raised her chin to look at her.

'It's over, Natalie. You know I won't give up until I get justice for Jamie. Why not tell us the truth?'

Natalie shook her head and blinked, a single tear rolling down her cheek. 'It was just a bit of a laugh to start off with. Then, Giles got pulled over for a routine traffic stop and they found that cannabis. Bloody idiot.'

Kay waited while the woman clenched and unclenched her hands, her jaw working.

'That bloody copper,' she finally spat out.

'Got a name?'

'Simon Harrison.'

'Go on.'

'I found out afterwards via a mutual acquaintance that he had a scheme whereby he'd trawl the system, looking for arrests of a certain nature. Not scumbags. People like Giles. Respectable.'

Kay let the irony of Natalie's assertion pass without comment. 'What did Harrison do?'

'He'd insist on reviewing the cases where he could see an advantage. Arrange to have the charges dropped in return for a cut – and introduce suppliers to more lucrative buyers for a finders' fee. Giles panicked – he couldn't afford to lose his job, so he agreed to Harrison's demands without consulting me and Jamie.'

'When did things start to go wrong?'

Natalie gave a bitter laugh. 'He went and fell in love, didn't he? Jamie, of all people. Of course, he wouldn't tell anyone her name back then, and I couldn't find out – I'd risk drawing attention to myself if I turned up at Deepcut out of the blue, even if Jamie was on deployment. That's the problem with being a twin, you see. People would notice, and then Jamie would've found out eventually that his sister was snooping around.'

She wiped angrily at the tears that reddened her eyes. 'Of course, when you turned up and said you were reopening the investigation into his death, I knew I had to find her before you got anything out of her. I think she always suspected I had something to do with it – that's why Jamie refused to tell me her name all those years ago. I just had to wait until you gave one of your pathetic speeches about the progress of the case and find out her name that way.'

Kay resisted the urge to lean over and shake the woman.

'What were you going to do to Amber?'

'I thought I might try to make it look like she was the one working with Jamie to supply the drugs.'

Kay frowned. 'How?'

Natalie swallowed. 'I doubt she's tried anything like cocaine in her life, not the way Jamie said she argued with him about it. I figured I could make her take a load of the stuff.'

'You were going to poison her? Give her an overdose?'

'I couldn't go through with it. I couldn't kill her.' She raised her gaze to Kay. 'Despite what you think of me, I'm not a murderer.'

'Really? Then perhaps you can explain to me why you left your brother to die.'

'What?' The woman's voice edged up a notch, her mouth agape. She swallowed. 'What do you mean?'

'Why were you going to see Jamie on the night of his death?'

'I just wanted to talk.'

'What about?'

'He did it on purpose, you know. Making sure that last stash of cocaine was found in the fuel tank.'

'How do you know that?'

'Because I do. He was already getting cold feet

the last time he was back from Afghanistan. You could see it. But, I'd sourced the best buyer we'd ever had – a higher price, everything. We just needed that one last supply, and he blew it. All those promises I'd made. It was an embarrassment. I was finished, as far as working in the City was concerned. I had nothing.'

'What did you do?'

'He wouldn't listen, don't you see? I had to convince him that he couldn't confess everything to his commanding officer later that week. He was going to ruin it for all of us. I tried to make him see sense, but then he told us that we were being unreasonable, and said he was going to go back to Deepcut that night and demand to see Stephen Carterton there and then and that he wouldn't take "no" for an answer. I was desperate – I thought if I spoke to him face to face, he'd see sense and keep quiet.'

'Were you driving under the influence of drugs?'

Natalie bit her lip, then nodded.

'I need you to answer out loud for the purposes of this recording.'

'Yes.'

'Did you have an accident while driving?'

'Yes.'

'Tell me.'

'I didn't mean to.'

'Tell me what happened, Natalie.'

'He was going too fast. I didn't see him.'

'Did you stop after the accident?'

'Yes.'

'What did you do?'

'I realised someone had swerved to avoid me. I thought he was okay. I stopped a few metres down the road, and ran back. I couldn't see him at first. Then I saw the number plate on the back of the bike, and—'

She choked out a sob, and reached out for the paper tissue her solicitor handed to her.

'I swear to God I didn't mean to kill him. I found him lying on the verge – his body was all twisted. I panicked. I knew I had to get out of there. If Mum and Dad found out… I didn't mean to kill him—'

'He wasn't dead, Natalie.'

The woman peered over the tissue at Kay, and cringed. 'What?'

'Jamie didn't die on impact. If you'd phoned for help as soon as you found him, he might've stood a chance. Instead, you were too focused on yourself and thought only of leaving the scene as fast as possible. Jamie died in hospital four hours later from his injuries. They might have been able to save him, if you'd helped.'

'No—'

Kay watched as Natalie slumped in her chair, the realisation slowly sinking in.

'I can't lose my children,' she wailed.

Kay closed the folder and rested her hands on the top of it before signalling to Barnes.

'Interview terminated.'

FIFTY-ONE

Kay pushed open the door to interview room one to see Giles Stockton lift his head from his hands, and noted that he appeared to have been crying.

She had little sympathy for the man, and avoided eye contact with both him and his solicitor while Barnes restarted the recording equipment and cited the current time.

'Mr Stockton, we'll be speaking to the Crown Prosecution Service with a view to bringing charges against your wife Natalie in relation to the death of her brother, Jamie Ingram.'

She heard the rush of air escape the man's lips as he slumped in his chair.

'I don't know what to say. What on earth do I tell Michael and Bridget?'

'I doubt very much you'll have the chance to speak with anyone by the time we're finished here. It was you who phoned Jamie that night, wasn't it? What did you talk about?'

He sniffed. 'He'd had enough. The fact that the drugs had been discovered in the Jackal's fuel tank frightened him – I think he knew it was the beginning of the end. He and Natalie had argued three days before when she had gone over to the farm. She had lost her job, and she had made promises to some people in the City who were expecting to take delivery of a large quantity of that last half kilo. She had done some sort of deal with them, something along the lines of if she provided the drugs, they'd provide her with a new role. She was desperate.'

'Are you a drug addict, Mr Stockton?'

He shrugged. 'I only had the occasional joint. Natalie was different, though. I think it's something in her personality – it could have been alcohol, food, anything – I think she's one of life's natural addicts. So, when Jamie told me it was all over, she panicked. She would lose her own supply, as well as what we were selling on. I tried to persuade him to continue, and we argued. He ended the call by saying that he was going to go back to Deepcut that night and demand to see his commanding officer to tell him what was going on.'

'And you told Natalie.'

'Yeah. She was staying at my flat in Maidstone, so she heard my end of the phone conversation, and when I told her what Jamie had said, she flew into a rage. You have to understand – she was Michael and Bridget's favourite. Yes, they loved Jamie I'm sure, but Natalie was their golden child. She couldn't bear for them to find out what had been going on. I tried to stop her, really, I did, but she was as high as a kite by then. She stormed out of the flat, saying that she was going over to the farm to talk to him herself.'

'What happened when she came back?'

Stockton raised his hands to his mouth and blew on them, as if he was afraid to let the words pass his lips. After a moment, he sighed.

'After an hour, I was beginning to panic. I knew better than to phone Jamie's mobile – the way our conversation had ended, he wouldn't have answered anyway when he saw my number. I tried phoning Natalie's number, but it kept going to voicemail. She came back about an hour and a half after she left, and I knew straightaway something was wrong. She was pale – so, so pale, and she was shaking; it was as if she were going into shock. I got her to sit on the sofa next to me, and eventually she told me what had happened.'

He broke off, and wiped the tears that streaked down his face.

'She'd been so high on drugs, she'd forgotten to switch on the car's headlights when she left my flat. It didn't matter driving through town and then out towards the farm; the streets are well lit until you reach the roundabout for the Leeds turnoff, and by then she was having enough trouble keeping the car on the road to notice. She said she didn't know how it happened – she was driving around the curve, then got blinded by a single light moments before she realised what had happened.'

He broke off, unable to speak as sobs wracked his body.

'Why didn't you report her to the police?' said Kay.

'I was too scared. I didn't want to lose my job. I was scared I'd lose Natalie.'

'Whose idea was the rehab clinic?'

'Harrison.'

'What?'

Giles sighed. 'I think he knew she was a high risk by then, incapable of anything except thinking about where her next fix was coming from. I think he was a bit afraid of her as well, and what she might tell people while she was high as a kite. He said he'd ensure Jamie's crash was ruled as an accident, but in return Natalie had to get cleaned up – and stay clean.'

'Did he blackmail you?'

'Money, you mean?'

'Yes.'

Stockton shook his head. 'The knowledge was enough. He knew about us, and we knew about his scheme to siphon off money from other drug deals going on around the county. You could call it a stalemate.'

'So, you, Natalie, and Harrison kept it a secret for all these years.'

'Yes. In a strange sort of way, it brought Natalie and me closer together. Of course, then we had even more to lose if anyone found out.'

Kay shook her head, and then listened to Barnes as he concluded the interview while she pondered her next task.

She had no idea how she was going to tell Michael and Bridget Ingram that they had solved the case, and arrested Jamie's killer.

FIFTY-TWO

Twenty-four hours later, Kay threw a pile of manila folders into the tray on her desk, and sighed.

After charging Giles Stockton with profiteering from the proceeds of money laundering, the sale of illegal substances, and perverting the course of justice by failing to raise his concerns about his wife's involvement in Jamie Ingram's death, she'd returned home close to midnight and had fallen into an exhausted sleep in Adam's arms, too tired to contemplate dinner.

For once, he hadn't nagged her.

He had forced her to eat two slices of toast before allowing her to leave the house that morning though, and she smiled at the memory.

She'd been fifteen the last time she could remember eating breakfast.

They had made arrangements that she would leave work early – she and Adam were to meet Rufus's foster family at a favourite spot on the Pilgrim's Way where Graham wanted to scatter the retired police dog's ashes. He wouldn't let Adam say "no" when he called round to their house on the way to take his daughter to school.

'He was one of the best dogs Kent Police had, so we'd be honoured,' said Adam. 'He had quite a track record for catching burglars, I hear.'

Graham had choked out a laugh. 'Just as well. He was useless at chasing rabbits.'

Kay rubbed at her right eye, and then pushed back her chair and wandered into Sharp's office.

There was still no word on when the DI might return to work.

Larch had been pleased with the result she and the team had obtained, and to Kay's amazement had personally congratulated her on a case well managed. His sabbatical had begun the day before, and the chief superintendent was rumoured to be keeping a close eye on the station in the absence of a senior officer.

Kay picked up a cloth and began to wipe away the scrawled notes from the whiteboard, removing the photographs she'd tacked up, and clearing the detritus left behind by her and the team.

A sense of pride filled her. It was the first time she'd led the team without having to defer to a senior officer, and she was surprised at how much she enjoyed the responsibility.

When she'd mentioned it to Adam the night before, he had rolled his eyes.

'Told you,' he'd said.

She grinned. Sometimes, she wished her emotions weren't quite so transparent. Often, her veterinary partner knew better than she did when it came to how far she was willing to push herself to get a result.

She turned at movement at the door, to see Barnes leaning against the frame.

'Do you and Adam want to come over to dinner tomorrow night? Sorry it's short notice, but I figured we haven't caught up properly for ages, and Emma's back from university. I know she'd be keen to see you.'

'Sounds great, thanks. What time?'

'About six suit you?'

'Fabulous. We'll bring the wine.'

She turned back to the now clean whiteboard, and wondered if Larch had brought Sharp up to speed with the events of the past few days.

Larch had elected to go and speak to the Ingrams with Kay regarding the arrest of their daughter, and in hindsight she'd been thankful.

Bridget had been distraught, and Michael had simply shaken his head before showing them to the door.

He'd called out to Kay as she'd been making her way to the car.

'Don't come back here again, Detective. You're not welcome.'

On the way back to the station, Larch had informed her that Giles and Natalie's children would be moving in with their grandparents for the foreseeable future.

Kay had watched the orchards pass the car window as they'd left the farm, and hoped the presence of children on the farm once more would go some way to ease the Ingrams' pain.

Her emotions had been buoyed by the news that Simon Harrison would now face further charges, and would receive a custodial sentence that would put him behind bars for a number of years.

She gathered the last of the stationery and case files into her arms before placing them on a trolley to be passed on to the administration team for processing, ignoring the persistent ache in her arm, and then frowned at the sound of a commotion at the main door to the incident room.

She pushed the trolley to one side, and stuck her head out of the door of the office.

Devon Sharp was making his way through the room – a slow process, as every officer greeted him, shaking his hand or slapping him on the shoulder.

She noticed that the beard had gone, and his hair was shorn back to its skull-hugging style that he preferred from his military days. His posture had changed, too. Where a few weeks ago she'd seen a shrunken man, he stood tall and proud as he laughed and joked with the team.

She leaned against the doorframe and watched as he crossed the room, her heart racing.

After all, her insistence at helping him had uncovered the truth behind the death of his godson, and destroyed the family of his closest friends.

Would he ever forgive her?

He seemed to make a point of ignoring her as he weaved between the desks, laughing with Barnes, teasing Carys, and shaking Gavin's hand, and paranoia clutched at her chest.

Had she made a mistake?

He turned then, and seemed to notice her for the first time.

She swallowed, and tried not to panic.

After all, with Larch on leave for the foreseeable future, DCI Devon Sharp was now her senior officer.

His face relaxed into a broader smile as he stopped in front of her.

'Guv.'

The skin at the sides of his eyes crinkled, and then he held out his hand.

'Good work, Hunter.'

She breathed a sigh of relief, pushed away from the door frame to his office, and then waved him inside.

'Welcome back, guv.'

THE END

FROM THE AUTHOR

Rachel Amphlett is a USA Today bestselling author of crime fiction and spy thrillers, many of which have been translated worldwide.

Her novels are available in eBook, print, and audiobook formats from libraries and retailers as well as her website shop.

A keen traveller, Rachel has both Australian and British citizenship.

Find out more about Rachel's books at: www.rachelamphlett.com.